The Ghost Guard

J. Cool

Acknowledgment

A big happy bold **thank you** for reading my first creation! Stories have danced around in my mind since I was a child and I finally decided to act on them. I didn't attend a fancy writing program, nor do I have the best attention to detail, vocabulary, or punctuation. I am sure you might find some errors in this very story, but I love a good adventure with wholesome vibes and family fun. My self-doubt is no longer going to hold me back and I hope this message empowers you to pursue your passions as well. Cheers to getting what we want and not being afraid to give it that deserving shot.

Countless individuals helped me edit and fine-tune this novel. I enlisted friends and family to read my drafts and supply their vision and insight. I am forever thankful to them. Pablo and Jackson would be proud of the support you showed me in making their story the best it could possibly be.

Cover Art by the amazing Hail Nowak (@allhaildesign)

Contents

Chapter 1: A Hero Is Born

"Hello, police?" Both of Mrs. Frizelia's hands were clutching the bright pink wall-phone receiver. She continued before the operator on the other end had a chance to respond, "My neighbor, Marie Elizabeth Dainger, has not left her house all morning. And I know this may not seem strange to you, but her son has a very strict schedule due to him being...well, you know... special."

"'Special, ma'am? Could you please elaborate?" The operator asked.

Mrs. Frizelia paused for a moment, debating on the right words to describe Frankie Dainger, the teenage boy from across the street. Her eyes jolted in different directions, her bottom lip swinging from side to side, competing in its own ping-pong match as she searched for the appropriate word.

"He has Down syndrome," Mrs. Frizelia said abruptly. "She is a single parent and I always told her that a woman shouldn't be alone for too long. The boy needs a father. His passed away some time ago, Lord rest his soul. Coast Guard mission gone awry. God bless our fallen heroes."

"We understand. Please state your name, ma'am," the operator said.

"Connie Frizelia. You should know who this is." Mrs. Frizelia responded.

"Thank you. I am transferring you to an officer now," the operator said.

"Ronald!" The operator shouted from the receptionist desk. "It's Mrs. Frizelia calling about an issue with the Dainger residence."

"Thank you, Jan. I will handle it," Officer Ronald said picking up his desk phone. "Hello, Mrs. Frizelia." I understand there is an issue at the Dainger residence? I went to school with the boy's father, Tim Dainger. May he rest in peace. This is Officer Ronald by the way."

Officer Ronald worked at the same police station since his junior year of high school. He and Tim Dainger were close friends back then. They had bonded over their dream of being in the military after graduation. Each wanted to join a separate branch and had a friendly rivalry going over which was more important, the Coast Guard or the Marines. By graduation, Tim went off to the Coast Guard, but Ronald's parents forbade him from going. They needed him to stay and help at the family store, Berdaldo's Grocer, named after his father.

Officer Ronald leaned back, belly protruding as he nestled his curvatures into the reclining pleather black office desk chair in the empty, white-walled police department.

"Oh, my stars, Officer Ronald," Mrs. Frizelia said. "I'm thankful it's you. Last time someone had picked up but never even said a word. I was talking to dead air." She expected everyone to know who she was and be at her beck and call since she made it her personal mission to know everyone else.

"Well, no need to worry now. We'll get someone over there posthaste," Officer Ronald said, now sitting up straight in his chair eager to send someone out to check on Marie Elizabeth Dainger and her son, Frankie. He picked up the phone to make another call and within the next ten minutes, two police cars were outside the home.

Mrs. Frizelia was waiting in her favorite chair near the window sipping her English breakfast tea. She enjoyed watching the neighborhood from it. It was perfectly positioned so that the whole street in front of her home could be viewed. She had put on a record to calm her nerves.

"Why don't you, you trust me!" she belted out the song lyrics to "Trust in Me," by Etta James.

Her hands were shaking as she brought the tiny teacup to her lips. A splash of it spilled on her fluffy crème bathrobe. The shaking of her right leg on top of her left surely didn't help steady anything. The right white slipper, oddly resembling the Easter bunny, was on the brink of being flung into the living room due to the forcefulness of her shaking. Her hair was nestled on top of her head and desperately battling for air beneath all the curlers.

She leaned forward peering through the closed white sturdy plastic blinds as the police knocked on the front door of the Dainger residence just across the street. There was no response for quite some time.

"Well, go in!" Mrs. Frizelia yelled to herself as if she were the commander of the mission. "I told you something was wrong. Just open the door."

The officers stepped toward the door, jiggling the handle, and opened it slightly. Mrs. Frizelia could see them going in one at a time with their guns drawn.

"Yes, there you go. Just walk in and find the boy. I'm sure whoever did it is long gone by now."

A few minutes went by, and Mrs. Frizelia grew worried. She started to bite her bottom lip anxiously. She stood up and fully opened the blinds for a better view, her eyes were glued to the Dainger's front door.

"If they don't come out soon, then I'm going to be forced to take matters into my own hands. I may be old, but I'm powerful," Mrs. Frizelia told herself as she pondered what the hold-up was.

"That's it, I'm going over there." She quickly stood up from her chair and shuffled to the front door. Her big white jacket with faux fur around the hood was on the nearby coat hanger. She threw it on, struggling to get her hands through the sleeves. She flipped off her slippers and forced on her rain boots. She was fully dressed but still felt as if something was missing.

"I need protection just in case. They may need back-up," Mrs. Frizelia said to herself still scanning the room with her eyes. She bent down a bit and saw what she had been looking for. Her wooden Louisville slugger bat with her name engraved on it. She remembered going with her father to the Louisville Slugger Museum & Factory when she was a child. Her father said the bat would always protect her and even taught her how to swing it for maximum damage. She pushed the coats aside that were covering it and grasped it with two hands.

"Yup, this will do the trick." Mrs. Frizelia swung open the door and immediately felt the cold chill touch her lips. She let out a shiver. "Whoop whoop, cold fingertips! Let's go, Connie. Keep it movin'," she said to herself through overdramatic chattering teeth. She closed the door and walked across the street towards the Dainger's house. The police were still inside, and the siren lights were on. She could see the other neighbors now turning on their porch lights to see what was happening. It wasn't a completely dark morning, but the gray overcast skies left the morning bland and discomforting. She approached the sidewalk, bat in hand, ready to defend herself in case things turned ugly. It began to rain, and the drops hit her bat first. She looked down in disbelief.

"Oh, perfect. The weatherman said it wasn't going to rain until after lunch," she said in disbelief. She put her fur hood on, and the rain began to fall stronger, slamming against the sidewalk in front of her. The strength of the drops had her so puzzled that she stared at the ground as they splattered. She lifted her head back up slowly and saw one policeman coming out of the house. Frankie followed behind him, wrapped in a gray blanket. Another officer helped him through the front door and down the concrete steps. Mrs. Frizelia stood there stunned and motionless as the rain drenched her jacket. Her eyes were fixed on Frankie, but he wasn't looking anywhere but down. She could barely make out his expression given the rain falling in front of her eyes but knew something was wrong. The officers walked Frankie to the police car and placed him in the back. Another police car pulled up with its siren lights a blaze but without the alarming sound. They didn't want to frighten the neighborhood. Mrs. Frizelia had still not moved from her rain-soaked position.

"Mrs. Frizelia, what are you doing out here? It's raining cats and dogs. Let's walk you back to your house," said Officer Ronald. She had not seen him before then so he must have just arrived.

"It took a while for them to come out. I was worried and came over to help. Where is Marie Elizabeth?" said Mrs.

Frizelia, still in shock and deeply concerned after seeing Frankie alone.

"Let's walk toward your home," said Officer Ronald as they pushed through the rain back to her front door. She opened it and stepped inside.

"I need to get back over there to take a statement from the boy. We found him alone in their upstairs closet sitting cross-legged and covering his ears, a slight sway had him rocking back and forth nervously. He wouldn't come out, so we had to lift him out. He's a heavy one too. Built like a linebacker. He seems really shaken up."

"Yeah, he's always been strong and such a momma's boy. Where is Marie Elizabeth? What happened to her?" Mrs. Frizelia asked.

"The mother has yet to be found. The doors were unlocked, and we found no signs of forced entry. She just disappeared," he said.

"That's not like her. That boy was all she had, her reason for living. Oh, I just can't bear this," Mrs. Frizelia was distraught and almost in tears.

"Ronald?" a voice shouted from across the street. He turned around and gave them a wave in agreement.

"Lock your doors Mrs. Frizelia and call us if you need anything. We don't know anything more at this moment. Please do send my regards to Mr. Frizelia as well," said Officer Ronald as he tipped his hat toward her.

Mrs. Frizelia sat for the rest of the day worried about Frankie and what might have happened to his mother, Marie Elizabeth. The police continued to search for her but were left with no clues or leads so they ultimately decided to close the case. They figured she left of her own accord.

Officer Ronald decided to take Frankie into his care. He couldn't be there for Frankie's father, Tim, on enlistment day but maybe he could help his son. Frankie had only a year and a half left until turning eighteen and the Ronalds were a well-known family around town. Mrs. Ronald also felt that the act of kindness would surely give people a reason to continue supporting Berdaldo's Grocer.

"Why, they even gave Frankie a job there," a customer would say.

Frankie aged into a fine young man by the town's standards. He was now 25 years old and still working at Berdaldo's Grocer as a bagger and stockboy. He had some money in savings and his own studio apartment above the store. This was his sanctuary, and he was free to decorate it however he pleased. He had pictures of his parents, his favorite action figures, unique mining tools, and pages from comics cut out and taped to the walls. People would always greet him and comment on his appearance. They used it to start a conversation given that they weren't sure how else to approach him.

"Why, Frankie, you have the most amazing green eyes just like your mother. She'd be very proud of you," said an elderly lady as he bagged her groceries.

"You could have been a linebacker for the Seahawks with a frame like that. Built like an ox, son. You know, your father played football back in the day," said Mr. Williams tipping Frankie $20 for bringing his groceries out to the car.

Frankie thought of his job at Berdaldo's as more of a necessity than a passion. He needed to keep a low profile and have a sense of stability in his employment for his true mission was much more profound. He had to dedicate every other waking hour to keeping the town safe. The weeks leading up to Halloween were always the busiest.

Chapter 2: Berrymount High's Elite

Frankie locked the front door of Berdaldo's Grocer from the outside and made his way to his bicycle that was chained up on the side of the building. It was his main form of transportation and best friend. The sparkling crimson red frame paired with top-of-the-line tires with deep grooving tread were his proudest modifications.

He put on his orange miner's helmet equipped with a light in the front and made his way to the town square. While on his journey, passersby would greet him as if he were somewhat of a celebrity. He would respond with a pleasant "hi" or "hello," never stopping to engage in further conversation. He never quite knew who to trust.

Unfortunately, the entitled elite of Berrymount High School didn't share the same keenness toward Frankie that the townspeople did. The ringleader, Brad, with his perfectly coiffed brown hair, and symmetrical face was the first to speak up. It was the week of Halloween and Brad's friend group was in the town square enjoying a few beers he had stolen from his parents' at-home bar. They were congregating around his white Jeep Wrangler. It had little doors with no windows and a hard-tan rooftop. It was a gift from his parents on his fifteenth birthday. It was beginning to get late and most of the town had closed their shops. Frankie rode his bicycle toward the

Craigsman Hardware Store for some extra supplies. Out of the corner of his eye, Brad saw him enter through the front door but could have sworn they had closed an hour ago.

"Why does Frankie walk around this town like he owns it?" Brad asked. His beer had one last sip in it, and he aggressively raised it to his lips, tilting his head back to catch every drop.

"*I like the way you brush ya hair, and I like those stylish clothes ya wear,*" Tod sang along to the radio playing "Ride Wit Me," by Nelly and City Spud.

"Tod, did you hear what I just said?" Brad asked.

"Well, you know the rumor," Tod responded. "They say he saves the town every Halloween from ghosts, or some crap like that." Tod was Brad's right-hand man and best friend since kindergarten. Tod, with one "d," was equally as arrogant as Brad. He was more brawn than brains. People would joke about his blonde hair having something to do with it.

"How can a retard save a whole town?" Brad asked. He crushed the empty beer can against his thigh.

Carmen, Brad's current love interest, (but oh-so-much-more than that introduction) interjected, "He's not a retard and you shouldn't say that word. It's demeaning and offensive. You're a jerk."

"Come on, Carmen, we're joking," Brad said. He hugged her from behind, and she pulled away from him. She wasn't used to being in the company of the "popular crowd," so she tended to overlook the mean things they said from time to time.

Carmen moved from Los Angeles, California to Berrymount, Oregon with her 11-year-old brother, Pablo, and father, Martin, in September just before starting her senior year. She never thought they'd leave their home, but fate had brought them to this moment. They used to be a happy, thriving family of four until breast cancer snuck in and slowly dismantled their lives. Martin ran a successful Los Angeles-based landscaping business for many years, but the medical bills became too much to bear. The tree-trimming industry was booming in the Pacific Northwest due to the fires, so he left his landscaping business for more lucrative offerings. Martin worked hard, long hours, and was always traveling, which left Carmen caring for her mother, and Pablo. Martin prayed that this new income would be enough for the doctors to get Veronica better, but nothing was working. Veronica Contreras Camarena passed away in her sleep on June 3, 2003. Carmen opened the bedroom door that morning and knew in her gut that her mother was now with the angels. Tears trickled down her cheeks, but she stayed still, staring at her mother at peace. She had an array of emotions from relief to longing and ultimately anger. She closed the door quietly and felt her legs give out. She crouched against the door and finally let out all her pent-up emotions.

Carmen and Pablo stayed with their grandma for the rest of

the summer, uncertain of what would come next. Martin had been successful in his new position and was promoted to supervisor, which required him to be in Oregon full-time. He was able to purchase a small home for his family and they all agreed on starting a new life together in Berrymount. Their mother had always loved nature and the trees so they planted her ashes in a tree in the backyard so that she could grow alongside them. Martin's mother, Cornelia, would also be relocating around Christmas to help take care of things. In the meantime, Carmen made a deal with her father to assume responsibility for Pablo and the home during those first few months. She knew her father was working very hard and the last thing she wanted was for him to be worried about them. But sometimes, she couldn't control her adventurous spirit.

Like that time, 13-year-old Carmen said she was staying with her childhood friend April but instead was doing keg stands at a house party of someone she didn't even know. She was curious about what kids her age did in other neighborhoods, so she took the bus to Fullerton and wandered into a high school house party. She blacked out by 11 pm and woke up the next morning locked in one of the house's guest bathrooms. She had lied and her parents did find out about it. They had called April's house in the early morning to see if Carmen wanted to go shopping. It wasn't long before the truth came out and the next few hours were spent in worry while everyone awaited Carmen's return. She had a guy from the party drive her home the morning after which made the whole scenario even worse. Grandma Cornelia ran out of the house swearing in Spanish as Carmen closed the passenger side door.

All in all, Carmen knew that things needed to be different this time. She needed to cling to her responsible and level-headed side, over her adventurous and risky one. She had always wanted to fit in and let it affect her judgment. She had a kind heart that she concealed with an attitude. The attitude wasn't the real her but more of a defense mechanism that way people never got too close. She hadn't yet realized that her authentic self was reason enough to be any story's main character.

Her beauty was unmatched. She had flowing dark brown hair just like her mother's. It was thick and healthy with an all-natural shine. She made sure to keep it long and used it as her superpower with members of the opposite sex. A slight flip of the hair was sure to catch the attention of any onlooker. Once the attention was grasped, her hazel eyes which changed color based on the sun and the colors she wore, were sure to get her whatever it was that she desired. She had never played sports but was blessed with an athletic figure and natural thickness in the chest and buttocks area. Strong, brown, petite, and compared to the other women in Berrymount, completely unique.

Brittany, the only other girl in the group, interjected, "Wouldn't it be funny if we played a harmless Halloween prank on Frankie?" Her face looked devious as her mouth cracked open exposing her tongue at the tip of her front perfectly straight white teeth. Her head wobbled ever so slightly as her thin bleached blonde hair bounced from side to side. Her glacial blue eyes glared firmly at the group waiting for their response.

Brittany was usually runner-up in beauty to every other popular girl in school no matter how much makeup she wore. She liked to keep her friends close, and her enemies in the gutter. Her father owned half the town, and she worked part-time at his realty company. She was so unhappy inside that the only way she knew how to get through the day was to be god-awful to everyone else. She honestly just missed her mother and wished she never left them. It was just her and her father now in their big, lonely house. He buried himself in work and other younger women as a distraction. She was practically alone most of the time. The lavish lifestyle and multiple homes never really mattered to her deep inside. Of course, none of her friends knew what she was going through. Men rarely asked questions anyway and that's all she hung out with.

Brad looked over at Brittany with curiosity. "What did you have in mind?"

"Well, Frankie is always going into that creepy abandoned house. Let's lock him in there on Halloween night at sundown. Obviously, he isn't that afraid of it, so it wouldn't be that scary for him. Just a little trick to our treat."

Tod interjected, "But what if he really does save the town every Halloween and we locked him up?"

Brad punched Tod in the arm. "You sound like an idiot! A retard saving the town? Get real. That's just some bullshit they say to make him feel special because both his mommy and daddy disappeared."

Carmen rolled her eyes in disbelief and grabbed her bag from his Jeep.

"See Brad, this is why no girls ever want to hang out with us. Just don't say the word, is it that hard to be PC?" Brittany said. Carmen was her only female friend, and she was starting to like the idea of having her around, so she tried to make the effort.

"PC?" Tod asked. He has no idea what Brittany was talking about.

"Politically correct, dummy," said Brittany.

"You're a douche. Hot, but a douche," Carmen said to Brad.

"Oh, come on, Carmen!" Brad yelled, throwing his hands in the air as she walked away. Carmen flipped him off and her long hair swished with her hips as she walked away.

Carmen crossed the street and was now on the sidewalk next to the closed storefronts. The streetlights flickered and the thick brown maple leaves that had fallen from the perfectly placed trees throughout the town square swirled around her due to the heavy gusts of wind. Her mind began to race as the chill of the night rushed through her body. She knew Brad was an entitled narcissist, but she loved the power that he carried. She felt a part of something and cared for when she was with him. She walked backward to see if they were still there and slammed right into an open door. She fell to the right and her whole body hit the concrete sidewalk. She crouched up a little bit and felt a hand land on her left shoulder.

"I'm so sorry. Are you okay?" an unfamiliar voice asked. "I didn't think anyone was out here, so I flung the door open. I feel so bad."

Carmen jumped back from the unknown hand quickly and into a sitting position so that she could move her hair from her face.

"Yeah. It wasn't even your faul..." Carmen tried to play it cool but couldn't even finish the last word because her eyes were now fully focused on the gorgeousness in front of her. His smile shined bright past his flawless dark complexion. His hair was buzzed short, dark black with a classy fade. He had a strong jawline and a soothing deep voice. His eyes were dark brown but big and piercing. He seemed so tall from where she was sitting. His broad strong shoulders blocked out the streetlight directly behind him. There was a kindness in his expression as his hand reached out to help her stand. She grabbed his hand and he sprung her up from the ground. She could feel his strength and immediately felt at ease.

"Do you want to come inside for a minute? I can get you some hot tea or something," he said.

"Um, sure, I don't even know you though. I mean, I could know you. I just don't. Right now." She forgot how to speak and couldn't form a correct sentence.

"Well then allow me to introduce myself," he said as he stepped back, fixing his apron, and wiping off his hands.

"I'm Dominik and you're Carmen. We go to the same school. You walk your little brother home from school every day and I pass by you on the bus."

He didn't mean to divulge all this information, but he couldn't contain his excitement. He remembered Carmen from the day she entered Berrymount High School but never dared to introduce himself.

Dominik was the strong silent type, but he was also a bit shy, so he mostly kept to himself. He and his parents moved to Berrymount when he was a freshman in high school. They thought he'd have a better chance at getting a college scholarship if he played for the Bearries, the high school football team. Their mascot was a brown bear in a blackberry costume. Dominik chuckled when he first learned of it. He has a great sense of humor but only lets it show for the people he trusts. He is now the starting running back and somewhat of a town hero because he scores touchdowns every game. His parents are a bit overprotective. They only want the best for him so keep him focused on school, work, and sports. They definitely wouldn't like him flirting with Carmen. Girls were off limits until a college acceptance letter arrived in the mail.

Dominik continued, "Wow, I sound like a stalker. Um, no, it's just that my bus just passes by…"

"You don't have to explain. I get it. Nice to meet you. So surprised I haven't seen you around school though," Carmen said.

"My parents keep me busy. Football, work, extracurriculars, and honor roll. Just look for lucky number 7 next time you watch a game. That's me," Dominik said.

"Oh yeah! I have seen you then. You're really good," Carmen said. She was still dizzy from the fall and felt as if she looked disheveled. She brushed a few of the hairs that had fallen to her face to the side behind her ear.

"Awe, I play alright," Dominik said. "Could be better," Dominik said.

"You know, my phone died, and I just need to charge it to make sure all is okay at home. My little brother is there alone watching old horror movies. He's kind of a freak but I told him I'd answer if he needed anything."

"Oh, of course, come in and let me get you some tea. It's cold out here," answered Dominik.

Carmen followed Dominik into the old diner. The floor was sparkling white, and it had old-style booths in a classic crimson color. She felt like she was transported to the 50s. The jukebox was playing "Reelin and Rockin," by Chuck Berry.

"Do you mind if I use the restroom?" Carmen asked. "I'm sure I look like a mess right now."

Dominik smirked shyly as he completely disagreed with that statement.

"You know, having just run into a door and everything," she said before he could respond.

"You could never look like a mess," Dominik interjected, looking over his shoulder at her as he filled her mug with hot water. He cracked a smile as she melted into a puddle of mush.

Carmen looked down, blushing then up again, moving her hair from her face with both hands. "Well, I see you're a charmer," she liked to push off compliments with humor.

The tea water was now spilling over the cup. Dominik laughed to himself, and Carmen took that as her cue to find the restroom. She got up from her chair and looked toward the back of the restaurant.

"It's the first door on the left, in the back," Dominik said.

"Got it. Thanks."

Carmen stood in the mirror staring at herself. She washed her hands and fixed the stray hairs that were out of place. She had all kinds of new feelings coming over her but tried her best to keep her composure.

"It's just a cute guy. No big deal. You aren't even official with Brad so it's not like you're cheating. Just typical you, having a fun time with someone helping you out. Get yourself together," Carmen told herself.

Dominik's appeal was that he was reserved, honest, strong, and different from the loud and emotionally challenged guys she'd usually go for.

Carmen exited the bathroom and sat down to her tea while Dominik finished his duties around the diner. Her phone was charging and luckily, there were no messages from her little brother, Pablo. She sat safe and sound enjoying a moment of tranquility. This was the first time in a long time that she felt at peace. She watched Dominik wipe down the counters and put away the various items. He did it with calmness almost like he was slowly dancing with whatever he cleaned.

"Do you mind if I put a song on the Jukebox?" Carmen asked.

"Yes, but only if it flows with our vibe. Here's a quarter." Dominik said, handing it over to her as she leaned across the countertop. Their fingertips touched and she tried not to lock eyes with him.

"This song is literally playing in my mind as I watch you work," Carmen said. She rushed over to the Jukebox and selected "In the Still of The Night," by The Five Saints. It started playing and she slowly swayed her hips back and forth before turning around to see his expression from her song choice.

"What? A classic. I honestly was not expecting this from you," Dominik said.

"I bet you thought I was going to play Destiny's Child or something," Carmen said with a laugh.

"Hey, I wouldn't have minded. Plus, you do give me that survivor mentality. How do you even know this song?" Dominik asked.

"My mom loved all types of music, and she would always be listening to something. I remember her bringing me to her dance classes and I would just sit in awe of how everyone moved to the music," Carmen said.

"That sounds like a beautiful memory," Dominik said.

She smiled back and continued sipping her team. She was hoping he'd get the hint and ask no follow-up questions. Dominik cleaned up some more and began locking up the diner.

"May I take you home?" Dominik asked.

"Well, you are technically a stranger, but I guess it beats running into weirdos if I were to walk home alone," Carmen said.

"Strangers don't go to the same school," Dominik said.

"You make a strong case," Carmen said. "Fine, you may take me home."

Dominik drove his father's all-black Chevy Suburban. Carmen climbed in and noticed the aroma of coconut and patchouli waft over her. It reminded her of a trip she took with her family before her mother got sick. They went to Puerto Vallarta, Mexico to visit her extended family and her mother taught her how to crack open a coconut. Carmen told her mother to drink it first because she thought it would taste bad. Her mother laughed and happily drank from it, a smile filling her face blissfully. She passed it to Carmen to try and sat anxiously in hopes of seeing a similar smile from Carmen when the liquid hit her taste buds. Carmen's face went from sour to sweet and her eyes grew big as she guzzled down every drop.

"So, where are your parents?" asked Dominik as he began driving her home.

"Well, it's kind of a long, sad story that maybe I'll tell you one day. But basically, my dad is on a work trip. He cuts trees and travels a bit. My grandma will be coming up over Christmas to live with us and help take care of my little brother Pablo," Carmen explained.

"But not to take care of you right?" he asked.

"I take care of myself. Always have."

"That must be hard. Everyone needs someone sometimes. What about your mom?"

"My mom passed away this summer before we moved up here. That was the long, sad story part that I'd rather not talk about," she said, staring out the window into the gloomy night sky past the big-leaf maple trees.

"Sorry to hear that. I bet she was just as sweet as you are." Dominik grinned. He just couldn't help himself.

"Okay, flattery sir, will get you everywhere. Thank you," she tried to respond fast with humor so as not to bring up past emotions and memories of her mom.

They stayed silent for a few minutes. Dominik turned on the radio and KC and JoJo's "All My Life" was playing. The lyrics reverberated throughout the car, *"All my life, I pray for someone like you, and I hope that you feel the same way too..."*

"Such a good song," Carmen said.

"How about this? Let me offer my services of being that someone whenever you need it. You call, and I'll be there," he said.

"That's very sweet of you. It would be nice to have someone here." She had only known Dominik for one evening but somehow felt more connected to him than any other person from school, including Brad. They pulled up to Carmen's house and Dominik put his number in her phone.

"I'm a man of my word," he said, handing the phone back to her. She looked at it and he had written: "Dominik, the Knight" as the name assigned to the phone number.

"Clever," she said with a side-eyed smirk. She climbed out of the car and walked to her front door, watching him from the doorway as he drove away. She originally thought moving would be horrible, but everything was turning out to be much more interesting than she had originally anticipated.

She walked in and Pablo was asleep on the couch. He had been watching an old horror werewolf movie and had spilled popcorn all over himself. She shook him awake and helped him to his feet. He walked half asleep holding her hand.

"Look, Carmen, I'm a zombie," Pablo said, still half-asleep in a groggy voice walking slowly in front of Carmen.

"You're a jokester even when you're asleep, aren't you?" she replied.

Pablo was one of those happy-go-lucky kids. He lost his mom and had to move away from his friends in California, but he still managed to find the joy in everything. Carmen tried to be more like her little brother. He was her best friend. She tucked him into his Ninja Turtle bedspread and closed the door quietly. The branches danced in the wind and the raindrops seemed to be falling in every direction. Pablo wasn't used to the sounds but found comfort in the droplets tapping on the roof. All the other ideas in his mind calmed down and he fell fast asleep.

Chapter 3: We've Got History

Frankie was the last person gallivanting through the drenched wind-torn town square that night. He did his best work when no one was around. He had to double-check the traps in Dr. Reed's Bookstore to make sure all was set up correctly for Halloween night. You see, the rumors around the town were true. He was, in fact, the protector of all on Halloween night. This particular night brought a new species of ghosts from the underworld into the real world via portals scattered throughout town and Frankie was tasked with closing them before the clock struck midnight. Frankie loved his greater purpose. He felt like Spider-Man making sure the town was safe, with great purpose comes great responsibility. He didn't ask for the task, but it was meant for him.

Frankie made his way to the back door of Dr. Reed's Bookstore. He looked around to make sure he was alone and then pulled a large ring of keys from his orange fanny pack. He had a set of keys for all the major locations in town and guarded them with his life.

He opened the door and looked as far as he could down the wooden staircase in front of him. It was completely dark, so he switched on his mining helmet's light. He always had to work with as little light as possible. He never quite knew whom he could trust given the ghost's unique powers. The old basement was dusty and smelled of mold. It mainly housed shelving and books too old to sell.

It began to rain outside, and the water leaked ever so slightly throughout the building. This creaky old store was not built on flat ground but a large rock. Within the rock formations was the first portal to the underworld. It shined brighter and oozed a dark purple slime as Halloween night drew closer. The portal was in its development stage and ripe for opening come Halloween night.

Frankie dragged the large spotlight from behind the racks over toward the portal. You see, the light combined with a certain type of obsidian stone was the only thing that could seal the portal and stop the ghosts from passing through. These ghosts were different in that they didn't possess humans but that of an extremely strong troll species. The trolls had been exterminated from Earth thousands of years ago, but their souls were very much alive in the underworld.

Cave people once roamed the earth and were free to enjoy the land and all its beauty. Sure, they had some enemies such as the dinosaurs, bobcats, and blood-slurping serpents, but nothing compared to the trolls their greatest adversaries. The trolls did not seek to enjoy the earth's flowers or swim in the crisp lake water but rather sought world domination. The trolls had bigger plans for humanity and the strength to battle them. Under troll rule, humans would become a food source, forced to procreate simply for feeding purposes.

The cave people realized this and made a pact to destroy every living troll. The cave people figured it was either humanity or the troll race, so they went forth with their plan and left the earth dripping in purple slimy troll blood.

Unfortunately, the trolls weren't finished with their plans for world domination even after being extinct. The trolls may have been taken off the earth, but they had unfinished business and were in the Underworld plotting their revenge. While there, they encountered the ghost population and began assessing how they too could return to the living world like them.

They realized that certain ghosts held the power of possession as well as re-entering the living world. However, they could only enter the living world through certain interdimensional portals on Halloween night when the sun began to set, one portal opening every hour. Each portal would remain open all year long if not properly closed. That is where Frankie comes in. He is the only one in Berrymount with the knowledge and ability to shut down the portals.

The trolls began kidnapping ghosts and testing out their powers as one. They had to become possessed by the ghost and overcome it to retain their troll selves as well as the ghost's abilities. In the end, a new species of ghost troll was created, and they are what haunts the town of Berrymount today. These ghost trolls can enter the portals to the living world and possess humans, taking on their shape, knowledge, and memories all while leaving the human inside powerless. Their larger plan was to travel through these portals, possess humans in powerful positions, and collect their young for consumption. They could also, however, stay in ghost form and haunt their enemies if they choose. Frankie had come across them in both forms.

Frankie positioned everything in the room so that come Halloween night, he'd be ready to shut down this portal before the ghost trolls squeezed through. Without him, every hour, six ghost trolls would pass through the six portals around the town of Berrymount. They would either haunt the town waiting for the next Halloween night in hopes of reinforcements or attach to a human life form seeking to establish some form of power in the community. Frankie was not about to let the world be taken over by these menaces. He owed it to his mother to be the protector. Unfortunately, he couldn't save her, so he made the safety of the town his life mission.

Frankie made his way out the back door of Dr. Reed's Bookstore and onto the dark wet street. He loved the smell of the damp October air. It reminded him of his father for some reason, but he never really understood why as he had never met him. He took a deep breath and felt the cold wet air pass through his lungs. At this moment he felt proud and well-prepared for what was to come. He was right on track to stop the ghost trolls from passing through the portals and giving his hometown yet another safe Halloween.

Chapter 4: A Cruel Intention

Carmen awoke to a sudden bang coming from downstairs. Her first inclination was to blame her little brother. He was well-known for causing a raucous.

"Pablo!" she shrieked and rushed down the hallway in her pajamas with one eye still shut from her slumber. She stomped down the stairs, almost tripping on the last step. Carmen entered the kitchen and flour covered the walls.

Pablo's face was barely visible through a cloud of white dust. He coughed and looked up at Carmen.

"Oh hiya, sister. I was just, um, practicing my baking skills. Home Ec sounds real interesting this time of year so figured I'd get a jump start," he said, weaving together a story of lies.

"Yeah right, Pablo. Are you building bombs again? What is all this mess about?" She began combing through pieces of wiring and battery within the flour.

Pablo was always up to some kind of trouble. He was fascinated by spy gear and wanted to be a detective when he grew up. He picked up the walkie-talkie and spoke, "Jackson, abort mission! Abort! Attempt failed!"

Jackson lived directly behind Carmen and Pablo. They were

both in the sixth grade and the same class. Jackson was intelligent, loyal, and loved a good joke just like Pablo. He lived with his grandparents and never talked about his actual parents. He was lanky with a full head of dark black hair that he didn't quite know how to style. His glasses made him look like a mad scientist.

Pablo and Jackson met on the school bus on Pablo's first day of school. Jackson was sitting alone in the middle of the bus. He wasn't, by fifth grade standards, "cool enough" for the back. Pablo never agreed with what others thought was cool though. He walked down the aisle of the bus searching for the best seat. He saw Jackson's Indiana Jones lunch box and stopped, now standing awkwardly in front of the unoccupied seat.

"Uh hi, where'd you get that lunch box?"

"My grandpa gave it to me. It's pretty much a family heirloom," Jackson said, still staring at the lunchbox in all its glory.

"It's so cool," Pablo said. "I wish I had one." He looked around the bus. The kids in the back were laughing and pushing each other.

"You, ah, mind if I sit next to you?" Pablo asked.

"If you want to," Jackson said surprised. He wasn't used to kids talking to him or asking questions. Pablo sat down and began telling Jackson why he loved Indiana Jones. Jackson agreed with everything Pablo said and thus, their friendship was born. They had become inseparable ever since.

"Okay, Pablo," Carmen said. "I don't care anymore, just clean this up. You're going to be in the seventh grade next year so growing up a little bit may not be a bad idea." She filled a glass of water from the kitchen faucet tiptoeing around the flour.

"And start getting ready for school. You're gonna miss your bus!" Carmen yelled as she rushed back up the stairs.

It was the week of Halloween and Carmen felt that everything was finally going well for once. She was fitting in and doing well in school. She thought losing her mom and moving would be the death of her, but she felt a weight had been lifted off her shoulders. She had been tasked with the care of her sick mother and the overall well-being of Pablo for many years. Her mom's death had been terrible, but she felt she was in a better place now. At least there was no more pain.

Her phone went off and it was a text from Brad. It read: "Good morning ;)"

She beamed with accomplishment. She managed to have the most popular guy in school like her after just a month or so of living in a new town. She put the phone down to make him wait a bit before responding and finished getting ready for school. She was just about to exit her room but spotted last night's clothes on the floor. She picked them up to place in the dirty laundry hamper but caught the tempting scent of coconut and patchouli. Dominik's scent still lingered on her red and black checkered flannel long-sleeve button-up. She flashed back to him spilling the hot water and the way he flushed with embarrassment. She chuckled to herself and tied the flannel around her waist throwing the other items into the hamper.

"Pablo, you better be heading out that door for school!" she yelled as she grabbed her school bag and folder.

"I'm going, I'm going!" he replied with a peanut butter and jelly sandwich in his right hand and his backpack dragging off his left. Carmen came down the stairs as Pablo was walking toward the front door.

"And don't drag your backpack, dude! Take care of your stuff. It's not like you have a lot of it," Carmen drilled. She always took on the parental role with him. She felt he needed to know that life wasn't fair, and nothing would ever change that. Pablo wasn't like the other more fortunate kids in the neighborhood and special treatment was not something he was going to ever get. He was more likely to be bullied and misunderstood than asked over for a cool kid's sleepover party. Carmen felt she had to toughen him up so that he could handle whatever came his way.

Carmen locked up the house and turned around, her dark hair glistened in the bit of sun peeking through the clouds.

Brad's Jeep was idling at the curb. She walked down the stairs confidently and hugged Pablo goodbye. Pablo stood as still as a statue. He didn't want her to know how much he cared but secretly he loved her more than anyone else in the whole world. He ran off down the street to meet Jackson so that they could walk to school together. Carmen turned toward Brad and walked toward the passenger side door.

"And what exactly are you doing here?" Carmen asked.

"Listen, I'm sorry for being a douche last night," he said. He reached his hand across the car towards hers that was resting on the windowsill.

"Don't apologize to me. You're the one who makes fun of people with intellectual disabilities to make yourself feel better," she retorted.

"Intellecta what now?" Brad asked in a funny voice.

"It's not a joke," Carmen said, pushing away from his Jeep and continuing walking to school.

He put the Jeep in drive and began to slowly follow her. "Come on, let me take you to school. You can even have control of the radio. We can listen to your bumpin' Mexican music," he said.

She walked slowly toward his Jeep passenger side door. "It's called reggaeton and it's better than that my dog died, girlfriend left me, drinking beers stuff you like." She grabbed hold of the roof and climbed in through the window area without opening the door. He let out an overdramatic gasp. This was exactly why he liked her. She put on her seat belt, plugged the AUX cord into her iPod, and played "Move Ya Body," by Nina Sky, Jabba.

She got comfortable in her seat and looked deep into his eyes. His face grew excited, and he leaned in as if he might get a kiss.

"And I'd also like a coffee before school," she said without acknowledging his kiss.

"See this is exactly why I like you," Brad said. "Keeping me on my toes."

She turned up the radio with glee and began slightly bobbing her shoulders from side to side to the beat.

Brad and Carmen arrived at school and walked toward Tod, Brittany, and the others in their group. They had their own spot in the school's quad where they congregated during breaks. Tod was napping in Brittany's lap, lying on his back and Brad kicked him as he arrived.

"Dude, wake up! Don't be such a pansy. You only had like two beers last night," Brad laughed. Tod rolled off of Brittany still half asleep and face down on the floor. He lifted his head and said, "Woah, I dreamed we actually pranked that special guy, and the world ended when you kicked me!"

"Like Frankie could actually save the world," Brittany said. "We really should prank him. I can get the keys to the old house from my dad's office. Tod and Brennon, you grab him on Halloween night before sunset right as he's leaving that Bernardo's store that he stocks cereal at. He gets off at four." She had lived in this town all her life and specifically decided to mispronounce the name of Berdaldo's Grocer.

Brennon interjected as he chewed his breakfast burrito. "How do you know all this? It looks like you have a crush on him or something." He nudged Tod.

"Brennon, you're so ugly you wouldn't even know what a crush is," Brittney lashed back. She paused for laughter, but no one did. "I'm just observant and know everything that happens in this god-forsaken town."

Brittany couldn't wait to get out of Berrymount. Her dad was developing a drinking problem over the heartache of her mother's departure. Brittany needed to stay strong for the both of them.

"Sounds like a fun night to me," Brad confirmed. Carmen turned away from the group and put on her headphones. "Pon de Replay," by Rihanna was now all she could hear. She had no desire to be a part of this conversation.

Chapter 5: Unhappy Halloween

It was Friday, October 31, 2005. Halloween had finally arrived in the town of Berrymount. Frankie awoke just before his alarm clock. He prepared for this day all year and looked forward to it. Today was also his 26th birthday. He was used to celebrating it alone, so he looked at himself in the mirror and said, "You were born for greatness. Happy birthday, friend." He put on his lucky superhero socks and dressed for work. Today was usually a day of stress and discomfort so whenever he felt overwhelmed, he'd look down at his socks for empowerment. He had to work at Berdaldo's Grocer from 8:00-4:00 pm before he could start his Halloween safety preparations.

Carmen was already up as well and styling her hair in her white bathrobe. She was a black cat for the school Halloween festivities and was in front of the bathroom mirror twisting her hair up into what looked like cat ears. Her lips grasped onto three bobby pins as her arms twisted and turned the hair into cat-eared origami. She had her all-black ensemble laid out on the bed, equipped with black lace-up combat boots. It was cute with a tiny bit of sensuality. The real showstopper of the costume was the fluffy kitty butt tail with a bendable wire inside of it that she could position ever so flauntingly. This could become an issue while sitting in class, but Carmen was ready to accept all the risks.

Everyone dressed up on Halloween in Berrymount. It was a town tradition, and you were severely judged if you didn't at least half commit to the event. She walked into Pablo's room brushing the left side of her hair as the right lay perched on her head perfectly styled. He was still asleep. She crouched down to the floor at the entrance of his door and crept on her hands and knees toward his bed. He was lying on his stomach tangled up in the blankets with drool spilling onto his sheets. She got to the edge of his bed and tickled his left foot poking out of the blankets. He wrestled around but did not awaken. She did it again but harder. He woke up a bit and she grabbed his leg hard, shaking and growling. He began erupting into laughter and fell right out of bed onto the floor.

"Carmen no! You ruined my good dream," he said.

He acted as if he were annoyed but honestly, the only thing that would annoy him is if Carmen did nothing at all. He loved being her little brother.

"I told you what would happen if you didn't wake up on time. I'm not always going to be here to make sure you are up and dressed for school. Now get your booty ready! It's Halloween," she said, climbing to her feet and shaking her booty as she left the room. She had to finish getting ready.

"And what are you wearing!? You look like a Mime," Pablo yelled with his face still planted on the floor. He laid there for a moment still waiting for his brain to awaken.

"Oh, it's Halloween. Jackson and I must make sure our costumes are in tip-top shape," he explained to himself as he climbed to his feet.

Carmen and Pablo loved Halloween. They had never lived in a city where it actually felt like autumn. In Los Angeles, they didn't have red, yellow, and orange leaves falling to their feet or cold gusts of wind anonymously pushing windows open. Los Angeles felt like one big warm sunny season all on its own. The brisk and quiet morning of the Pacific Northwest had a way of awakening the spooky Halloween spirit in them.

Pablo came into her room dressed in his costume a few minutes later.

"Ha!" He shouted as he jumped into her doorway to surprise her.

"Ew, you didn't even shower Pablo. All the kids at school are going to think you're the smelly boy from LA who doesn't wash!" Carmen said.

"Uh, relax! I'll shower! I just wanted to show you, my costume. Do you like it!?" he asked, awaiting his sister's excitement.

He wore dark blue jeans with a matching blue tie, his favorite white Vans shoes, a black bowler hat, and a long yellow raincoat. A glass marijuana pipe resting in his mouth.

Carmen began to chuckle. "You look like a knock-off Sherlock Holmes!"

"You guessed it right! Jackson and I couldn't find the fancy tan trench coats, so we settled on the yellow raincoat. Because you know, it's rainy up here so it fits," Pablo said.

"I love it. You definitely can't take this one to school though. Let's find you a magnifying glass or something," she said as she took the pipe out of his mouth and hid it in her desk drawer. She put her arm around him and led him out of her room toward the bathroom.

"How did you find all these awesome props?" she asked, somewhat concerned but with a fake upbeat undertone so as not to make him feel uncomfortable.

"Jackson and I raided Dad and his grandpa's closets. We have a major case to solve," Pablo said.

"Sure thing, Sherlock. Just make sure you put that stuff back when you're done with it. I wouldn't want a call from Jackson's grandpa."

"We will. Don't you worry your pretty self," Pablo said.

"I'm happy you have such a good friend here," Carmen said.

Pablo smirked and was about to respond but a loud yell came from downstairs, and their eyes lit up.

"*Chiquitos*!" said a strong cheerful voice from downstairs. It was their father, Martin.

"Where are my childrens!?" Martin yelled. They hadn't seen him in many weeks and ran downstairs jumping into his arms.

"Missed you, *Papá*!" They both said as they squeezed him.

"Me too. I couldn't miss out on seeing you both in costume for Halloween!" Martin said as he held them tight. He pulled away and kept them at arm's length to see what they were wearing.

"Carmen, looking beautiful as ever, and Pablo... You need to shower, *mijo*. Detectives are supposed to be debonair! You can't be smelling up the school. Come to me when you are fully dressed, and I will give you some of that expensive cologne that your Tia got me for my birthday last year."

"Yahoo! You the best, *Papá*," Pablo said, jumping up as if he were trying to tap the ceiling just before running up the stairs to finish getting ready. He was so excited that he tripped on the stairs but quickly stumbled to his feet.

"I'm okay!" He yelled back.

Martin smiled and let out a chuckle. "You little rascal!"

Martin loved being a dad but unfortunately missed a lot of Pablo's upbringing due to his job. Pablo was very young when Veronica got sick, and Martin was the breadwinner for the family, so he was usually at work. He had hoped this would be a new chapter in their life and that he could get back to being a dad. Martin focused his attention on Carmen.

"*Mija*, now I know I said you look beautiful but also please not too much make-up. And you can't wear just a bathrobe to school. You need something more creative! And a jacket. This is not enough clothing. The boys up here are a bit different from what you are used to. You can't just knock them for being locos and get away with it," he said.

"*Papá, no te preocupes*. This isn't my costume. Plus, you know the cousins taught me a thing or two about dealing with entitled rich boys," she responded.

"Yes, that is what I am afraid of. One lawsuit away from taking our *casita*," he said, kissing her forehead. "Just make good choices. Remember to ask yourself, '*Que haría Veronica?*'"

"She'd have boys buying her lunch every day, start a dance party in the courtyard, and run the debate team," Carmen smirked.

"*Exactamente*. Now add a bit of my ambition, and heart to that and you'll be just fine," he said as he hugged her.

Carmen headed back up the stairs to finish getting ready for the day.

Martin looked around at his new home and his eyes brightened. It was the fresh start his family needed. He knew his love, Veronica, would have been proud. He headed into his room to unwind from his travels.

About an hour later, Martin was relaxing on the couch when a honk came from outside. Martin peaked his eyes through the blinds to see who it might be.

"*Carmencita*? Why is there a boy in a Jeep honking outside our house? His car has no windows!" Martin yelled.

Carmen ran into the room from the kitchen with her hands full and in a hurry.

"What would Mamá do right?" she asked before kissing her father on the cheek.

Martin wasn't even sure how to respond. His eyes squinted and his mouth pursed. He looked at everything she was carrying and said, "Now, I don't know why you just don't use a backpack! Your folder, sweater, and purse stuff could all be in one bag."

"Fashion Papá, it's a choice," Carmen responded with sass. She looked in the mirror and began rearranging her items so that she looked more organized.

"Pablo, you're going to be late. You better hurry," she yelled up the stairs.

"Carmen, you need a jacket, and that outfit is too tight," Martin said.

"*Si, ahorita,*" she said, grabbing her unusually small black pleather jacket from the coat rack.

"*Te amo*," Carmen said as she shut the door. She stopped for a moment to breathe and collect her thoughts. She walked down the stairs toward the Jeep.

"Are you always this punctual?" she said as she opened the door.

"Only when I really want something," Brad said as he put his tongue between his teeth, raising his eyebrows.

"You're crazy. What are you supposed to be anyway?" she asked while staring blankly at Brad's outfit. He was wearing a bomber jacket, with a white V-neck, dog tags, and aviator glasses.

"It's not obvious…" He shot her a glance with an eye roll.

Carmen shook her head and popped a stick of gum in her mouth acting as if it weren't important.

"Maverick? Top Gun?" he responded with his mouth still slightly open, and his right hand waving in the air waiting for her reaction.

"Oh yeah. I see it now. Cool," she said, shaking her head in agreement. She tried to be as convincing as she could be even though she had never actually watched the movie.

She plugged in her iPod and selected the song "Turn Me On," by Kevin Lyttle. She put the radio volume just loud enough to drown out his presence so that she could enjoy the trees dancing in the wind outside her window. Brad started to drive, and she put her arm out the passenger window to feel the cool air rushing through her fingertips. She let her hand flow with the wind like a hawk gliding through the air.

Everyone at school was in the full Halloween spirit. The front door to the school was decorated with a large spider hovering over it with fake purple and lime green cobwebs trailing down to the door handles. The loudspeaker was playing "Monster Mash," by Bobby "Boris" Pickett and The Crypt-Kickers. Carmen was feeling spunky and began moving her shoulders ever so slightly to the beat as she entered. She felt right at home.

Brittany spotted Carmen from down the hall and

approached.

"Hey girl, love the cat fit. So, meow," Brittany said looping her arm through Carmen's.

"Thanks. Just something easy, ya know," Carmen said. "I know people are pretty into Halloween here." Carmen didn't care very much for Brittany but loved having a "cool" friend, so she embraced her touch as if they had been friends forever. Maybe Brittany would grow on her. They continued walking down the hall together.

"Oh yeah, it's a must for this season's fashions," Brittany said. "Hence, my outfit."

Brittany was dressed in a provocative witch costume complete with a smokey eye, bright purple sparkly lips, a witch's hat, and a tight little black dress. Everyone stared as the girls walked down the halls, and Carmen felt empowered.

"Remember to meet up right after school at my place for our secret pre-game party," Brittany whispered with a wink as they unlocked their arms to head into class.

Carmen couldn't remember what she was referring to but liked that she belonged to a group of friends so smiled and nodded in agreement.

Frankie was eagerly waiting for the clock to strike four so he could head directly to his tree fort to prepare for the night. He had been distracted all day. He was now on his last task of restocking the canned food shelf at the back of the store. He turned around with two cans in both hands and bumped right into Brad.

"Sorry," Frankie said as he regained his balance still holding the cans tightly in both hands. It was a miracle none had hit the floor.

"You will be," Brad said as he continued walking past Frankie toward the back exit.

Frankie had only seen Brad a few times around town. Brad would frown or make an ugly expression toward him which Frankie tried to ignore. He was used to people looking at him strangely, so he tried not to think too much about it. They had never formally met. Frankie finished stocking the cans and hustled to the back office to gather his things. He packed up his bag and scurried to the back door. He swung it open and walked out into the alleyway. The cold night hit his face and two hands landed on the backside of his shoulders gripping forcefully.

"What's up, retard? Time to oink like a pig," the voice came from behind and as Frankie went to turn around, he was pushed up against the brick wall by two other people wearing pig masks.

"No, wait," Frankie called out but was gagged with a blindfold. Two people were holding him by each shoulder. The person who seemed to be the leader was the first to come behind him.

"Haven't you always wanted to become one of us?" The voice said devilishly just before thrusting a similar pig mask over his head. Frankie began to grunt and could not see out of the mask but still managed to headbutt the ringleader in his plastic pig nose. A slight snort came out from the person behind the mask.

"You piece of shit," the leader cried out as he put his hands under the mask to catch the blood. Frankie broke free from the person on the right grabbing the other with both hands and head-butting him. He made direct contact with the pig impersonator's bottom lip.

"Dude, what the hell!" said the impersonator as his hands went up to his lips to make certain he wasn't bleeding. Frankie was now free and began to run down the alleyway. He turned around to see if the masked pig kidnappers were chasing him and ran smack into a large white van. Frankie was knocked off his feet and hit the ground slamming his head on the pavement. The pig impersonators caught up and kicked Frankie while he was on the ground.

"It didn't have to be this violent, but you just had to headbutt us-didn't you?" the ringleader said as he walked up to meet the group fixing his mask, blood still on his fingertips from the initial blow.

"Get him up!" the pig-masked ringleader ordered. The others grabbed Frankie as the ringleader opened the sliding van door. "Throw him in."

The doors closed and the van sped off. While in the van, the pig impersonators tied Frankie's hands behind his back and moved to the front of the van. They took their masks off and began conversing among themselves. Frankie could hear them laughing and making jokes. He figured they were kids from the town and amateurs, unlike the actual troll humans he had encountered before. They would definitely not be speaking in high school slang or making fake fart noises. He wondered what he had done to them to be in this van.

"Guys, shut up!" Brad shouted at the others in the van.

"You know he can still hear us, right?" he whispered pointing to Frankie in the back who was sitting against the van wall silently cross-legged. The driver, Dillon, turned up the car stereo and they drove in silence nodding their heads to "Give It Away," by the Red Hot Chili Peppers.

They pulled up to the abandoned house just before sunset and right on time. The house was an old Victorian style with a large stoop and a broken porch swing. It used to be painted in a mix of sky blue and white. Now it was grayish in some areas from the dirt with chipped paint and broken windows. Many of the town's youth would throw trash and bottles in the yard. The weeds grew tall in between the broken glass and rubbish. Brad and his band of misfits definitely contributed a few beer cans and broken bottles to the house decor.

Brittany was outside waiting, still in her witch costume, unlocking the chain-link fence. She motioned them to pull to the back of the old creepy house. The van passed her by, and she peered into the window to see if she could catch a glimpse of Frankie, but the windows were too dark. She made a sinister expression showcasing her excitement over pulling it off and closed the gate. She strutted to the back quickly. Her high heels slammed against rocks and dirt, as she rushed to catch the sight of Frankie being pulled out of the van. The guys held him by both arms and dragged him up the backstairs into the cold empty house. Frankie didn't make a noise so as not to draw the attention of the neighbors. If it was the troll humans who kidnapped him then he didn't want anyone else in danger. The wind blew through the inside, and the house creaked loudly. A door slammed closed, and Tod squealed.

"It's just the wind!" Brad yelled annoyed at the stupidity of his friends. "Put him in the living room and let's meet back outside. It's creepy in here."

They dropped Frankie to the floor next to a large armchair covered in a white sheet. All the furniture was covered in sheets, and dust. They sloppily tied him to the arm and leg of the chair and made their way to the backyard to meet up with Brittany.

Frankie was sitting cross-legged trying to figure out where

he might be. He knew the whole town by heart, and based on travel time, knew he was still within a few miles of Berdaldo's Grocer. He calmed his breathing down and began to listen to the sounds around him. His hands were tied behind his back to the chair, but he could still reach the floor. He outstretched his fingers to feel the floor's solid wood texture. The splinters tried ever so hard to wedge between his fingertips. It was cold and he could feel the dust between his fingers. He listened to the sounds of the wind creaking through the house. The fireplace whistled and the old, ripped curtains rustled with each gust of air. He took a deep breath through his nose and let out a loud sneeze from the dust. He knew exactly where he was. But why would they bring him here? Were they working with the ghost trolls? Frankie had to think of something and fast. The abandoned house was also home to the first ghost troll portal. Luckily, he was in the right location just without the necessary tools from his treehouse hideout. He could still see light coming in from the windows through his pig mask, but it was getting darker by the minute. He had to stop the portal from opening or else the first six ghost trolls would enter and begin their evil plan.

Brad and the others stood outside celebrating their kidnapping achievement.

"You guys were late by a few minutes. I hope you weren't seen," Brittany said.

"He was a little harder to subdue than we thought. Why is he so strong?" Tod asked.

"That's just because you're weak. You guys couldn't even hold him in place," said Dillon who was driving the getaway van.

"Shut up. Now my damn nose is busted open. Better not be broken," Brad muttered as he pushed Dillon. Brad also didn't think Frankie would be as strong as he was. Although he wouldn't admit it, he had been a little bit afraid.

"So, Brad, where is Carmen? She said she'd meet up to get ready with me after school but then never texted back. Why do you always pick the flakey ones?" Brittany asked.

"She said she had to make sure her little brother was safe and then would stop by before taking him trick-or-treating but guess not," Brad replied.

Chapter 6: Let There Be Ghosts

Carmen arrived at the old house and peered over the gate to see if she could see anyone, but it looked deserted. She heard rustling in the nearby bushes and stepped back a bit worried that it might be some crazy stray dog or wild creature eager to attack her. She stared harder and could see two dark figures through the leaves.

"Alright, clowns, come out before I claw your eyes out," Carmen said.

The whispers grew louder, and Jackson crawled out first with his hands up in the air. "Okay, lady, don't scratch us to death," he pleaded.

"Detective Jackson! What are you doing here? And I know that must be Pablo still hiding in there. Pablo, get your little booty out here right now," she said.

Pablo crawled out sheepishly and climbed to his feet.

"We were just protecting you, sis. You said you'd be right back, and all horror films say that you're not supposed to say that. We had to make sure you'd be okay," Pablo explained.

"What horror films are you watching, Pablo?" Carmen asked.

He shrugged his shoulders.

"Well, see? I'm fine," Carmen said. "I was going to come right back and take you both trick-or-treating. I just had to do one thing. Now, please go wait a few houses down, and I'll be there in fifteen, twenty minutes."

Pablo and Jackson both shot her confused looks. Carmen knew they weren't going to leave her without more information, so she lied.

"Fine, fine! My friends are right inside here, and they were going to tell me the spots around here with giant candy bars! It was supposed to be a surprise, but obviously, you both can't be fooled," she said, now texting on her phone telling Brad to come outside to meet her.

"Oh, okay then!!" Pablo yelled with excitement. "We will be right over there practicing our karate moves in case you need backup."

"Yeah, please go karate chop each other for a minute in front of the church right down there. There is some type of outdoor kids' event with games. Here are a few bucks and take my phone just in case. I'll be there in ten minutes," Carmen said as she handed them her phone and ten dollars from her black leather fanny pack.

The boys grabbed the items excitedly and ran toward the

church. Carmen walked back to the fence and saw Brad walking down the driveway. She didn't want to be a part of any stupid prank that could get her into trouble. She just wanted to say hi and leave.

"Hey, come in. We did it," Brad said quietly as he unlocked the gate.

"No, I don't want any part of this. I just wanted to tell you that in person. My brother is down the street, and I need to take him trick-or-treating," she explained while backing away.

"Hey no, don't go. I really want you to be in my crew of friends, and this will make it so much easier for you. You can just wait outside. Then I'll buy your little brother all the candy he wants. My parents have king-size bars at the house," Brad grabbed Carmen's hand pulling her against his body.

"We can get our own candy. I don't need your parent's executive sizes. They probably like Almond Joys and coffee candies," Carmen said, pulling away from his hand. A lot of the things Brad said annoyed her. He said things in a way that made it seem like she needed him.

"At least come say hi. Everyone wants to see you. Just come in for a few minutes and wait outside," Brad said. His facial expression grew into that of a sad puppy dog.

"Ugh fine, but I don't want to see the poor kidnapped guy.

I'll just say hi to everyone and then meet my little brother and his friend. I don't want them out there alone," Carmen said.

"Of course, princess. Just for a minute," Brad grabbed her hand and led her through the gate locking it behind them. They made their way to the back of the house and Brittany stared judgmentally at Carmen.

"Guess you'll only come if a man asks you," Brittany said to Carmen without looking at her. Brittany didn't have many female friends. She was genuinely excited that she and Carmen seemed to be getting closer.

"Yeah, I'm sorry. On babysitting duty, unfortunately," Carmen answered apologetically.

"Okay, well, you're here now. Come see what we got today," Brittany said as she walked toward Carmen and linked arms somewhat pulling her up the back stairs.

Carmen glanced back at Brad and mouthed the words, "Help me." He rolled his eyes and motioned his head toward the house as a way of saying, "Go inside."

The girls entered the house through the creaky wooden back door, which led directly into the kitchen. The draft from inside crashed into her body as soon as the door opened, and chills ran through her. The kitchen was filthy and looked as if a hurricane had passed through it. Old dishes, leaves, and trash were scattered throughout the floor. The air was damp and black mold-like patches covered most of the walls. The smell of trash, feces, and wet German Shepherd hung in the air. The path to the next room was clear though as if someone had done it on purpose.

"This house is so gross and creepy. Why would you guys want to come here?" Carmen asked.

"Patience, my pretty," Brittany said as they walked slowly into the main room.

"For this," Brittany said, motioning to Frankie. He was quietly sitting on the ground still tied to the chair in his pig mask. Carmen's eyes lit up in a frightened way. She stepped back almost ready to run away.

"Oh no," Carmen said at the sight of Frankie. "Why would you all do this? I'm going to untie him. I honestly thought it was just some drunken joke when the idea first came up."

"It's just a Halloween prank. He doesn't even think like us, so probably won't remember it," Brittany explained as if Carmen's concerns were irrelevant.

"Well, you guys have your fun then. I don't want any part in this and need to watch my brother," Carmen said as she slowly walked backward out of the room.

She ran right into Brad's arms. He gave her a big hug, almost lifting her off the ground. "You can't go yet. The fun is just getting started." The other guys followed in after him, and the door was barricaded.

Frankie could hear the whole conversation and realized that these actions were not the inner workings of the ghost trolls. It was much too messy and emotional. If he didn't get out of this scenario quickly then the whole city would be in jeopardy. The first portal would release six ghost trolls into the town. They'd most likely need to eat. Children are their specialty, but they'd settle for a teenager in a pinch. They would quickly take over the town's most powerful. Then begin their plan for domination.

Frankie's stopwatch went off with a five-minute warning. "Beep, beep. Beep, beep." Frankie began to groan and tried to break free from the chair.

The group could hear him rustling. Carmen pushed away from Brad. "This is inhumane. I'm untying him." She headed into the room. Frankie flailed on the floor in a panic.

"It's okay. It's okay. I'm going to untie you," Carmen said, trying to calm Frankie down. She took off his pig mask and mouth gag.

"The town is in danger. We must shut down the first portal now or suffer the consequences," Frankie pleaded with Carmen.

"Okay, sure. Whatever you need. I've got you now," she said, helping untie his hands. She figured he was in shock and speaking in gibberish. The others waited in the doorway watching and laughing.

"See he's crazy," Brad said jokingly to the crew. "It's just a joke man," Brad yelled to Frankie.

"No, you don't understand. We are all in danger. I must get to the basement to shut down the portal," Frankie explained.

The house began to shake, and a purple glow came up from the floorboards. Everyone stumbled and grew fearful.

"It's an earthquake! Take cover!" Brad yelled as he braced himself in the doorway.

"What the hell kinda witchcraft is this, Brittany?" Dillon asked.

"What!? I don't have anything to do with this. My outfit is just a costume. I'm not a real-life Sabrina. Let's get out of here!" Brittany said, running to the front door. She pulled hard, but it was locked. "This door won't open!"

Carmen finished untying Frankie and he climbed to his feet.

"We have to get to the portal in the basement. We may not be able to shut it now, but we can at least try to stop the ghost trolls from passing through. Follow me!" Frankie said.

The rest of the group was in shock and either standing under the doorway with Brad or flailing around the room still deciding what to do.

"Carmen, come to the doorway. It's the safest spot!" Brad said.

Carmen looked at him and then at Frankie and for some reason, she believed Frankie was telling the truth. Frankie was now heading down to the basement. She followed him down the small creaky staircase. It looked as if someone had set up a whole workstation. There were maps on the walls and tools organized on the workbench. Someone had been down there working on things before. It didn't look abandoned like the rest of the house.

"Quick! Plug this into the wall," Frankie said, handing the cord to Carmen. Without hesitation, she crawled on her hands and knees plugging it in under the workbench. A huge light illuminated pointing at a rock formation that was oozing purple slime and a glowing fluorescent soft purple light, the house still slightly shaking.

"We don't have much time, but obsidian rock and light will stop the ghost trolls from coming through the portal. This necklace may not be enough but it's all we have since I didn't get to go to my treehouse for supplies. This is the key to everything."

He took off the dark brown leather necklace. It had an arrowhead pendant at the end, which was about the size of a quarter and made from obsidian rock. Frankie held the necklace in front of the light, and the rock let out a blackish-green light at the portal. The purple ooze began to harden, and the intensity of the necklace grew. Frankie was shaking and reached his other hand up to the necklace for more support. Carmen tightened her grip on the light, moving it closer to the necklace and the portal hardened, slowly closing.

Two purple formations shot out from the portal into the room knocking Carmen, Frankie, and the light fixture to the ground. Frankie held tight to the necklace as he hit the surface. The purple formations swirled around in the basement looking for an exit causing a tornado-like force around the room. Frankie climbed to his feet picking up the light fixture from the floor and forcing himself closer to the portal with the necklace. The light fixture shook from the force of the swirling purple formations.

"We're too late! They're here! Help me close it!" Frankie said in a panic, yelling at Carmen. Carmen regained her strength, brushed off the dust from her fall, and stood up, steadying the light fixture. A loud noise came from the basement window. Pablo and Jackson were trying to kick in the window.

"Carmen, we got you!" Pablo screamed, kicking the window in.

"No! Don't come in here. Run home!!" Carmen screamed to the boys.

Just then the window shattered. The two purple formations shot through the window into the night knocking the boys back onto the ground. The boys hurried back to the open window throwing their raincoats over it and crawling carefully through the broken glass. They rushed to Carmen to help hold the light steady.

"Detectives and Black Cat, listen to me," Frankie said, still holding the necklace in place and staring intently at the three. "You must get to my treehouse in the forest past the old mill factory. It will tell you all you need to know. This doesn't stop here. Not now, not ever. I will stay here and get this closed."

"What are you talking about!? What the heck is going on and who are they? Or what are they?" Carmen yelled.

"They're ghost trolls! The town is in danger and..." Frankie was unable to finish his sentence. Two long, hairy purple translucent ghost troll arms stretched out of the portal and caught hold of Frankie's t-shirt. They began to pull him into the portal headfirst. Carmen and the boys screamed. Pablo grabbed Frankie's left foot, which was still out of the portal to pull him back in. Jackson grabbed the right foot and used all his weight to help pull. Frankie's head and left arm were now back in the room. His right arm still inside the portal continued being pulled in.

"Take the necklace and get to my treehouse! It's the only way," Frankie yelled.

Pablo motioned to Jackson to grab Frankie's left leg as well and Pablo shimmied up Frankie's body to meet his outstretched hand. Pablo grasped the necklace. Frankie was whipped out of Jackson's hands and pulled fully inside the portal.

"No!" Carmen screamed as she pulled Pablo back from the portal right before he was about to fall inside. A purple formation grew tall floating directly in front of the portal. It was an eight-foot-tall hairy ghost troll with big facial features that were almost translucent and floating. The ghost troll reached out to grab Jackson. Pablo used the necklace's sharp point as a knife to slice its outstretched hand. It let out an eerie screech and its translucent skin began to fizzle and melt away leaving an open gash. Jackson grabbed the light from Carmen and Pablo held the necklace up to try and stop the ghost troll from approaching. It began to sizzle from the beam.

Two more purple formations shot out of the portal and went through the ceiling above. Brittany, Brad, and Tod came rushing down the basement stairs.

"What the heck is that chasing us!?" Brittany asked. She tripped on the final stair and crashed to the ground. Tod went to pick her up, but the ghost troll grabbed him by the waist and pulled him into its mouth. It swallowed him whole in one gulp. The ghost troll looked up toward the window and in a flash of purple light was gone.

"Tod!" Brittany screamed. "That thing just ate Tod!" She went into shock and began to kick and scream on the floor. Brad grabbed her and they made their way to the open window. Brittany was hysterical. "That thing literally ate Tod," she said. Brad helped her up to the window. She climbed out, the skin of her hands ripping open from the broken glass.

Brad yelled to Carmen motioning her to climb out the window before him. "Carmen let's go! We have to get out of here!"

Carmen glanced over at her brother and Jackson, still trying to fry the ghost troll in front of them. Brad yelled out to her one more time, "Let's go!" but she turned to her brother and ran over to help steady the necklace instead. Brad was too fearful to wait any longer. He jumped up to the window and climbed out to safety.

"It's not working!" Pablo yelled as he held the necklace up in the light pointing it toward the blinded ghost troll in front of him. The light was holding the ghost troll back, barely damaging it.

"We need more power! Like a laser beam," Jackson said frantically. Pablo and Jackson looked at each other and the idea hit them both at the same time.

"Our detective magnifying glasses!" They shouted in unison.

Jackson placed the magnifying glass behind the necklace. It let out a dark beam of green light, which blasted the ghost troll on the left side. The ghost troll grabbed its shoulder and let out a screech.

"Yes, guys! Keep doing that. It's working" Carmen exclaimed.

The boys used the light, necklace, and magnifying glass to blast the ghost troll as they moved back closer to the window. Carmen grabbed the magnifying glass from Jackson with the large light resting against her body.

"Jackson, you go first! Climb out and help Pablo after," she said. Jackson carefully climbed out and immediately turned around to offer his hand to Pablo.

"Go Pablo," Carmen said, nudging Pablo away from her. He climbed up and grabbed Jackson's hand. Carmen used all her strength to throw the light at the ghost troll and the boys pulled her out together. She fell directly on them onto the grass outside the window.

"Okay, what just happened!?" Carmen said in shock.

"Well sis, it looks like we just let loose a couple of teenager-eating ghosts if you ask me," Pablo said. He climbed to his feet, brushing off the dirt, and putting the necklace around his neck.

"Jackson, you were almost ghost dinner," Pablo said.

"You totally saved me from fighting off that beast like a Three Musketeer," Jackson replied.

"Anything for my brother from another mother." Pablo put out his right fist with his thumb extended, staring directly at Jackson. Jackson extended his left fist with his thumb extended to meet Pablo's and upon connection, they launched it outward like a rocket.

"Wow, you guys have a secret handshake?" Carmen asked.

"No, it's just something we do," Pablo explained.

"Yeah, like a right-on buddy kind of thing," Jackson added.

"Okay, so a secret you go bro-friend thing, got it!" Carmen replied.

Jackson and Pablo stared at her as if she were crazy and tried to cross their eyes while making silly faces. Carmen pushed Pablo into Jackson in a loving sibling type of way. They nearly fell over but quickly regained balance. Pablo began to pace around the grass. Jackson walked over to the window to reassess the basement.

"Now, how do we stop them?" Pablo asked.

Just then, another purple formation shot out of the house's side windows and into the atmosphere. Jackson dropped down to his knees ducking for cover just to be safe. While on the ground, he grabbed both of their coats and shook the glass off. He put the coat on carefully, readjusting his tie and bowler hat.

"Now, where do you think it's going?" Jackson asked as he walked over to Pablo handing him his coat.

"Not sure, but it looks like we just got our first case, Detective," Pablo said, shaking the coat off once more before putting it on.

"Oh no, Pablo. This isn't one of your adventures. That guy from my school got eaten. We need to get to the police. Frankie kept saying all these crazy things about a treehouse and saving the world," Carmen said.

"Yes, Carmen. Probably because he knew something we didn't. If he told you to go to the treehouse and not the police, then there must be a bigger scheme going on here."

"Exactly!" Jackson said. "Frankie obviously knows something we don't. He had heavy-duty equipment in that abandoned house's basement. It must be down there for a reason." Pablo nodded his head in full agreement and they both stared at Carmen.

"Yes, I hear you, but that thing ate Tod. We need to get to the police. I'm pretty sure his dad is a police officer. He would probably want to know this classified information, don't you think?" Carmen asked.

"Agreed. Let's assess the police department's interest in the case," Pablo said.

"Give me the cell phone Pablo," Carmen said as she smirked a bit at his seriousness over being a detective.

"No way. We are not calling the police or that wimpy Barbie doll guy you were with!" Pablo said.

"Yeah, Carmen," Jackson said. He climbed out of the window instead of helping us. I sure hope he isn't your boyfriend. You should be with someone more cavalier." Carmen was always impressed with Jackson's words of wisdom and vocabulary. She let out a slight chuckle. They both kept her lighthearted even in chaos.

"You are wise beyond your years Jackson. Of course, I'm not calling Brad. It's someone else you don't know." She grabbed the phone and began to dial.

"Well, he better not slow us down," Pablo said.

"He has a car, Pablito." The boys looked at each other and nodded in agreement. The phone rang and someone on the other end picked up. "Hey...So it's Carmen. The random girl you met at the diner. Remember when you said you'd be that one person for me when I needed you?"

The voice on the other end could not be heard by the boys. They looked at each other suspiciously trying to figure out who it could be.

"Well...the time has come. Can you pick us up at that creepy abandoned house everyone in school avoids? We need a ride to the police station."

Chapter 7: The Slime Thickens

The boys were sitting on the curb outside of the house examining the arrowhead necklace with their magnifying glasses. Carmen stood pacing back and forth thinking about the events that had just unfolded.

"It's obsidian rock guys," she said to the boys who were completely enthralled by the necklace.

"It has some secret type of magic. I wonder how we trigger it," Pablo said.

"The obsidian is the magic. Or at least that's what Frankie said to me before he was dragged into that freaky monster portal," Carmen said.

The boys looked up at her with sad expressions. She wanted to say something like, "I'm sure he will be okay," but she didn't even believe that herself. A flash of light hit the boy's eyes and a black Suburban pulled up to the curb. The window rolled down and the sounds of "Put It on Me," by Ja Rule and Vita filled the air.

"Your chariot, my lady," Dominik said. He turned the stereo down so that he could give Carmen his full attention.

Carmen smirked, "You are the best. Thank you so much for

coming." She looked back toward the boys and motioned them to get in. "This is my friend, Dominik. He's a good guy and will take us to the police station."

"Oh, we got some detectives on the case already. Climb in guys," Dominik said to the boys still sitting on the curb. The boys climbed to their feet and walked toward the Suburban. Jackson went to the passenger side back seat door following Carmen.

They both opened their doors and locked eyes, "I see you found your knight in shining armor," Jackson whispered.

Carmen smiled. "Just get in the car." She couldn't believe how fast Jackson had become a part of their little family. It was like they had known him for years. She climbed into the car and the boys began to tell Dominik the whole story. They would act out the movements as they told Dominik about how Pablo saved Jackson's life and how Jackson pulled them both to safety through the broken window. Dominik listened as if they were telling a made-up tale and asked them questions to show Carmen that he was engaged in their epic adventure. She knew it sounded ridiculous but let them continue until she could have a heart-to-heart with Dominik.

"Well, this adventure needs to be shared with the town sheriff," Dominik said in a sarcastic yet believable way giving a wink to Carmen. He turned the stereo up again and "21 Questions," by 50 Cent and Nate Dogg was playing.

"So, you're a star athlete, work hard and listen to good music? I'm impressed," Carmen said.

"Yeah, I make my own mixed CDs. Music is really important to me. I pretty much always have something playing," Dominik said.

"That's cool. I use an iPod, but maybe you could make me one of your CDs. It would be fun to see what songs you think I'd like," Carmen said.

"Will do," responded Dominik.

His cheeks puffed out and he smirked at her. He looked like a happy chipmunk. He wanted to see her expression and briefly glanced her way. She was staring at the moon. He thought about how grand their memories together were already becoming. Carmen was also thinking about him and how nice it was to have someone there for her. She saw his hand on the shifter and placed hers on top of his. Her hand was cold and slightly shaking. Her small fragile fingers were half the size of his. Dominik flipped his around to hold hers properly. He knew she needed him to be the strong one at this moment.

Pablo poked his head into the front seats breaking their connection. "Why does your car smell like coconut?" he asked.

Carmen chuckled at Pablo and pulled her hand away from

Dominik's.

"Get your seatbelt on Pablo. This is serious," Carmen said.

Sirens began to sound behind the Suburban, and police lights flashed violently. Jackson and Pablo climbed onto their knees looking out the back window.

"Can we trust them?" Jackson asked Pablo.

"Not in the slightest. Be on your guard," Pablo responded.

"Please continue driving, and follow all directions given." A voice came over the patrol car's loudspeaker, but it sounded almost crackly and out of breath.

"See, Pablo! Now we are going to get a seatbelt ticket. Sit down right and put your belt on pronto," Carmen scolded.

"Well, now we don't have to drive all the way to the station," Jackson said with a bit of relief.

"Alright, guys, it's okay. Everyone just sit back and keep cool. We will be very cordial with the officer and follow all directions. No one reach for anything and just stay still. Let me handle this," said Dominik. His parents had taught him early on what he needed to do when approached by police. He realized he had a car full of minorities and that they may be met with a bit more questions than usual.

"Please continue driving until directed otherwise," a voice said over the loudspeaker. The siren lights and sound were now off, but the spotlight was kept on the Suburban. They continued driving for a few miles and were now completely outside of the neighborhood. They were surrounded by large maple trees whose branches extended into the sky above the road. There was only a streetlight every few miles that illuminated only a sliver of the road.

"Why are they making us drive this far out?" Jackson asked.

"I don't know, but let's just follow their directions. When we stop, we will find out why, and everything will be okay," Dominik said.

"Turn right at the next street," said the voice over the loudspeaker.

"No, no, why?" Dominik grew worried. His eyes jumped to every mirror of the car trying to see what he could make out from the police car. The chorus of "Suga Suga," by Baby Bash and Frankie J was playing in the background and he turned the stereo knob down aggressively so that he could fully concentrate on the situation.

"What, what's wrong?" Carmen asked. She turned her full body toward Dominik in fright. She was now looking out the back window.

"Well, there is nothing down that street. It's completely dark and just a forest," Dominik said. He turned right and drove the Suburban a bit more before the voice came over the loudspeaker again.

"Pull over here," the voice said. It was now even more crackly and hoarse as if they had a frog in their throat.

"Okay, something isn't right," Carmen said. "This is way strange. Do the police act like this up here?" she asked Dominik.

"No, not at all. Wait, that is the sheriff's patrol car," Dominik said as he pulled over to the side. He had a better view of the SUV behind him now.

"The Sheriff is Tod Johnson's dad, right?" Carmen asked Dominik.

"Yeah, I'm pretty sure. Why?" Dominik said, checking his driver-side mirror to see if anyone was getting out of the sheriff's patrol car.

"Because that ghost thing ate Tod in that abandoned house," Pablo blurted out.

"Okay, you all have to stop with this tall tale. If a kid actually died in that house, then that makes us the primary suspects," Dominik said. He was no longer looking out of his mirror but starting directly at the boys in the back seat. He began to sweat.

"Why is it so darn hot in here?" Dominik asked.

"No, no Dominik, Brad, and Brittany saw the same thing. I'll explain later," Carmen said. She began touching the air conditioning controls to blow some cold air on Dominik.

"Maybe the sheriff thinks we killed Tod," Jackson said thinking out loud to himself.

"Those people are not your friends Carmen," Dominik said. "They will throw people like us under the bus the second they can."

"Okay, I can't even talk to you about all that right now. What are we going to do here?" she asked him.

The unknown voice continued over the loudspeaker, "Everyone out of the vehicle."

"Okay, relax everyone. We will just get out calmly and follow the directions," Dominik said.

"It's a trap. I'm not doing it," Pablo said.

Dominik turned around and shot a disgruntled look at Pablo. Pablo and Jackson looked at each other and Pablo shook his head side to side, mouthing the word "no". His eyes were wide open, and he exaggerated the ending "o."

Jackson looked at Dominik and said, "Me neither. This seems fishy. Even the voice sounds suspect."

"Okay, fine. I will get out and go talk to the sheriff," Dominik said.

"Something is weird about this Dominik," Carmen said.

"Don't worry I'll handle it. You all just stay in here."

Dominik got out of the Suburban, cautiously closing the door behind him. He put his hands up with his back toward the patrol car.

"Sir, I am complying. My hands are up, and I am walking backward slowly toward you," Dominik said. His body was stiff, and he made certain that every step was done slowly and calmly.

The loudspeaker blared, "Yes, come to us, and then we will get the others."

Dominik grew more suspicious of this supposed "sheriff" and his tone. He felt it sounded almost villainous. The two figures got out slowly and made their way to the front of the police car. They were both tall, almost 6'5 standing directly in front of the headlights. They had slight hunches and their bodies seemed disproportionate. Pablo and Jackson were peering out of the back window, studying the scene.

"Uh, Pablo, what do those look like to you?" Jackson asked.

"Definitely not the fine police officers of Berrymount. It's those things from the creepy house. Why are they so big and ugly?" Pablo asked.

"Frankie called them ghost trolls. We have got to get out of here," Jackson responded.

"On it," Pablo said climbing toward the front seat. Dominik was still walking backward toward what he thought were police officers.

"I am complying officers. Don't shoot," Dominik said.

"Pablo, hurry up! They look like they are gearing up to eat Dominik!" Jackson said from the way back of the Suburban peering out the foggy window to get a better look.

"What are you guys talking about? Pablo, what are you doing?" Carmen asked.

Pablo climbed over the center console and made his way to the driver's seat strapping his seat belt in. "We've got a date with fate, sis," Pablo said as his hands clasped the steering wheel firmly.

"No, no Pablo. Get in the backseat. This isn't a joke," Carmen said, strapping her seatbelt knowing he wouldn't listen to her.

"They are getting hungry, Pablo! They are going to eat him! On my count!" Jackson yelled from the back, his face and hands glued to the window. The ghost trolls repositioned their stance into attack mode and were ready to feast on Dominik who was still walking slowly back toward them unaware of the real danger at hand.

"3...2...1...Punch it!" Jackson yelled as he jumped from the trunk to the backseat lying down flat on the seat. "Bracing for impact!"

"Wait, what? Pablo don't!" Carmen yelled as if she were at the top of a drop tower roller coaster waiting to fall 300 feet to the ground. Her arms were firmly at her sides, her head flush against the headrest and braced for impact.

Pablo popped the shifter into reverse and stretched both of his legs out to hit the gas. He firmly held the steering wheel in a steady position. The engine revved and wheels spun out just before launching the Suburban backward passing Dominik walking at its side and slamming the ghost trolls into the hood of the police SUV!

SMACK, CRUNCH, POP!

Purple slime splattered across the vehicles from the beasts directly after impact. Both cars were now heavily dented from the crash. The police SUV began to smoke.

Jackson poked his head into the front seats. "Is everyone okay?"

Carmen was still in her stiff upright position not moving just in case this ride had one more twist or turn.

Dominik slammed his palms into the driver's side window. "You all are crazy! You just killed two police officers and wrecked my dad's baby. We are in serious trouble. What were you all thinking?"

Pablo climbed up from the floor to the seat completely ignoring Dominik. His eyes locked onto Carmen. "Now might be a good time for that heart-to-heart with your boyfriend."

She gave a concerned but understanding look back at him, nodding her head in agreement. She somewhat enjoyed hearing her little brother say the word boyfriend. She opened the passenger side door and put her foot on the ground. A large slimy purple hand grasped her sneaker and pulled the rest of its mangled body forward using her as a crutch.

It let out a growl, "Leaving so soon? We still haven't had dinner."

Carmen shook her foot intensely trying to break free from the ghost troll's grasp.

"Carmen, what is it? Kick it off," Pablo yelled.

The ghost troll's other hand grabbed her calf muscle, almost pulling her out of the car. She grabbed onto the handle inside the Suburban that was just above where the door would close, finally realizing the importance of the handle. She braced herself to start kicking. The ghost troll's mouth grew wide and began pulling itself closer to take a bite from her ankle. She jolted her foot back and forth trying to break free. The ghost troll had her in his grasp and she was unable to kick him directly in the head.

Jackson jumped from his seat to the center console to see if he could help.

"What do we do?" Jackson yelled to Pablo.

"Cheer her on," Pablo answered.

"Let's go, Carmen. Kick him in the dome!" Jackson yelled.

"Brother said knock him out!" Pablo added on.

Carmen continued flailing her foot and trying to kick at the ghost troll, but she couldn't make contact.

Dominik leaped into action as soon as he realized what was

happening. He ran over kicking the mangled bleeding ghost troll directly in the face like it was the winning goal at a soccer match. It let out a yelp like a hurt coyote and released Carmen's leg.

"Direct hit!" Jackson yelled.

"And the crowd went wild! Aghhh," Pablo said.

Dominik helped Carmen gain her balance and lifted her back into the car.

"Sis, you survived," Pablo said.

"Very brave indeed," Jackson said.

Dominik closed the door gently and peered into the window to make certain that she was safe. They locked eyes and both forgot where they were for a moment. Her luscious chestnut hair covered parts of her face and her hazel eyes, that seemed to be sapphire blue in this moment, peered through it to connect with Dominik's. She thought he looked so strong out there and the butterflies in her stomach began to flutter. Unfortunately, their gaze was broken as Dominik was pulled to the ground by the ghost troll. They began to wrestle, and his clothes were now covered in purple ooze. The dirt stuck to his shirt as they rolled around. The ghost troll had Dominik pinned and was getting ready to feast. The passenger side back door flew open, and Pablo launched onto the ghost troll's back with the arrowhead necklace in his right hand stabbing at its neck repeatedly. Purple ooze shot out in all directions and dripped down Carmen's window. The ghost troll fell to the right of Dominik and Pablo was still on its back.

"I got you, Pablo!" Jackson yelled. He jumped out of the Suburban and pulled Pablo from the ghost troll's back. They stood there for a moment in awe staring at it.

"You slain that valiantly my friend," Jackson said.

Carmen got out of the car to help Dominik up. She put him into the passenger seat and shut the door behind him.

"I wouldn't stare too long, boys. It may just come back to life. Let's go," Carmen said.

She watched as they climbed into the back seat and went over to the driver's side. She wasn't sure how badly Dominik was hurt and decided to drive.

Carmen kept trying unsuccessfully to start the engine. The car was having trouble turning over.

"What's wrong, sis? Never learned how to drive?" Pablo asked.

"Still better than you at it, little brother," Carmen said.

She cranked the engine once more but nothing.

"There's something on the roof!" Pablo yelled.

"It's making its way to the front of the car," Jackson said.

A large purple hand with claws smacked the front glass window startling her. She screamed which prompted everyone else to as well.

"The one Pablo mutilated is also awake and looking this way! Lock the doors!" Jackson yelled.

Dominik hit the lock button on his door. The beast tried to open the door but could not enter.

"It's headed to the front!" Pablo said.

The two ghost trolls were now slamming their fists into the roof and hood of the car.

"You got this, Carmen. Nice and steady with finesse. Try saying some nice words to it like my dad does," Dominik said.

"Your dad can talk to cars?" Pablo asked slightly joking.

Another fist slammed into the roof of the car leaving a huge dent. It startled everyone in the car.

"Ok, sweet coconut dream-cicle, start for me baby," Carmen said endearingly.

"Ba ha ha, what did you just call it?" Pablo asked.

"Clever, so clever. I felt that," Jackson said.

The engine revved up loudly.

"I can't believe it actually worked," Carmen said.

"All it needed was some love," Dominik said.

She slid the shifter into drive and floored it, slamming into the ghost troll in front. It immediately fell to the floor.

"Seatbelts everyone," Carmen said. She revved the engine as she ran it over. The boys were thrown out of their seats.

Pablo climbed onto the center console switching the music from CD to radio. It was on station 97.6, "The Real Rock and Roll", and "Black Betty," by Ram Jam was playing. He cranked up the volume.

"Such a good song!" Pablo yelled as he climbed back to his seat quickly fastening his seatbelt. Jackson was already safely buckled in.

"Time to rock out!" Jackson said, holding up a rock and roll hand gesture. Pablo hooted loudly because he loved how much of a dork Jackson was.

A pounding came from the roof once again directly above Jackson.

"There is still one on the roof!" Jackson yelled.

"Juke 'em, Carmen!" Pablo exclaimed.

Carmen swerved the car to the right and left now going almost 50 MPH down the abandoned dark road. They hung on strong and punched at the roof.

The chorus for Black Betty rolled along.

"Whoa Black Betty (Bam-ba-lam)
Go Black Betty (Bam-ba-lam)
She's from Birmingham (Bam-ba-lam)"

"Carmen, hit the brakes and at the last second slightly turn to the left. It will fling it right off," Dominik said.

"Genius," Carmen said.

"Yeah!" Jackson and Pablo yelled bobbing their heads to the heavy metal tunes still faintly audible through the car speakers.

Carmen looked straight ahead and adjusted her body to

have full control over the vehicle. Dominik turned the volume back up on the stereo. Carmen released the gas pedal and hit the brakes. The Suburban jolted to a stop, and at the last moment turned the wheel slightly to the left so that the vehicle was almost perpendicular to the road.

The ghost troll on the roof had no chance. It tried to hang on but lost balance once the car turned and flung directly into the nearby woods just as the song on the radio ended.

"Heck yes!" The boys cheered high fiving each other.

"You did it, Carmen!" Jackson said.

"You see that thing fly?" Pablo asked. Pablo and Jackson high-fived and began discussing how the whole event went down.

Dominik grabbed Carmen's hand.

"It really did. You saved us" Dominik said while staring at her intensely.

"Thanks for your help. You were right," Carmen said.

Pablo undid his seatbelt and stood up patting Carmen on both shoulders.

"You are the coolest sister ever. I just love you," Pablo said.

He was now fully embracing her.

He went back to his seat and fastened his seatbelt once again. She fixed her hair placing the fallen parts over her right ear and repositioned her body once again to drive. She let out a slight smirk. The Suburban sped off into the night leaving the injured ghost trolls in the dust.

"Now, can we please go to the treehouse?" Pablo begged.

"Yes, precisely. We really should have listened to Frankie from the beginning," Jackson said.

"Dominik, are you badly hurt at all?" Carmen asked, ignoring the boys in the back.

"Yes, just a couple of scratches," he said, inspecting his wounds and cleaning himself up with his dad's handkerchief from the glove compartment.

"That thing didn't bite you, did it?" Jackson asked.

"Yeah, because you know… if it did then we may need to kick you out of your own car. Can't risk you turning into one of them and eating my sister," Pablo quickly chimed in.

"He's not a monster, you guys," she said, shooting them both a motherly scolding look through the rear-view mirror. "Please just let the grown speak," she said to them.

"You sure you're okay?" she asked, grabbing Dominik's arm. He looked up and they locked eyes for a few brief seconds.

"Don't crash us now," Dominik said.

"Oh, sorry," Carmen said. "Yes, I'm the driver. I think we should go check out this treehouse. Frankie was very specific about us going there. I trust him."

"If that is what your gut says, then let's do it," Dominik said. "I trust <u>you</u>. And at some point, y'all are going to have to fill me in on what's really going on."

"That's what we," Pablo said pointing to himself and Jackson, "the true detectives, had been saying the whole time."

"Hey, didn't Frankie mention the Old Mill Factory and the treehouse hideout being somewhere behind there?" Carmen asked.

"Yes!" Pablo and Jackson said in unison.

"Let's head there then," Dominik said.

The group drove toward the factory and on the way started to see cars heading to the high school.

"That's so weird," Carmen said. "Halloween night and

everyone is heading to the high school. Shouldn't people be trick-or-treating or putting their kids to bed?" She drove slowly past the school.

"You may want to get us out of here before we are spotted by the police again," Jackson said. "We did just wreck a police vehicle."

"Faction Jackson back at it again," Pablo said.

Their chatter grew silent, and everyone seemed to be in their own heads processing all of what had just happened. All that could be heard was an unexpectedly louder than others radio commercial.

"Come on down to Big Jolly John's Steaks & Bakes this holiday season. Where friends become family and food becomes favorite. Located off I14 and Lexington Dr."

The booming voice of the overly cheerful gentleman on the radio startled Carmen out of her thoughts and she quickly began flipping through the stations.

"Thank you!" Jackson yelled. "I can't stand that commercial. It doesn't even make sense. It's like they just wanted the f's to rhythm. It should say, 'Our food becomes your favorite,' or something similar."

"It's supposed to be fun, Jax!" Pablo said. That's the reason why. When it's fun it doesn't have to make sense."

"For some people, yeah. For others, it's just annoying," Jackson said.

"And this is why we are best friends. Opposites attract! When I am with you, I just keep learning."

Jackson nodded his head in agreement.

Carmen had finally found a radio station worth listening to and "Butterfly," by Crazy Town was playing. She looked in the rearview mirror and saw the boys bobbing their heads to the beat. Jackson and Pablo couldn't help but sing along to the chorus.

"Come, my lady, come, come, my lady, be my butterfly," Pablo sang.

"Suga, bay-bay," Jackson finished the line.

Chapter 8: Frankie's Hideout

They arrived at the Old Mill Factory. The place was deserted, wild overgrown weeds now covered most of the entrance. It was a murky night and only one lone flickering light partially illuminated the front of the factory.

"This place is really creepy," Carmen said. Why would he put his hideout here?" She drove slowly along the dirt side road toward the forest area just behind the factory.

"He probably knew no one would come searching back here," Dominik replied.

Pablo and Jackson were now both behind the passenger side seat staring out of the window inspecting the factory for clues.

"You guys are all excited about this. Aren't you scared?" Dominik asked.

"Actually, just more curious," Jackson said.

A barrier stopped them from continuing down the dirt road. They stopped the car for a moment to assess their options.

"We have two different paths here. One looks like a road for emergency vehicles and the other a hiking trail," Carmen said.

"It doesn't look like anyone has been down either of these paths in years. All the plants are overgrown," Dominik said.

"It's the road less traveled. I just know it," Pablo said.

"Yeah, but how do you know that? Maybe he wanted to be closer to the main road," Carmen replied.

"News flash, sis. Heroes don't think like that. Why would he want people to see his secret hideout that protects the whole town from a ghost troll infestation?" Pablo responded.

"There could be another trail up ahead though off that emergency road," Dominik said. "Why not inspect the whole area and then double back?" Carmen loved that Dominik could hold his own in these conversations and keep up with her eccentric little brother.

"Listen, new guy, you're cool and all but you're not a detective," Pablo said, patting Dominik on the shoulder.

"Actually, Pablo, I see both points," Jackson said. He picked up his backpack in search of communication devices. "It may be best if we split up to check out both paths. We can use the walkie-talkies." He also pulled out two flashlights.

"Where did he get a backpack full of gear?" Dominik asked Carmen.

"Always be prepared but never make it obvious," Jackson responded.

"Hey! Those scary movies say never split up," Carmen said. "Plus, as if I would let you two go wandering off into that forest alone. No, not happening."

"Paleasseee. As if we'd..." Pablo said motioning to Jackson, "...leave you two love birds alone...in the woods...and without a proper detective. I will go with the new guy and Jackson goes with you."

Carmen rolled her eyes, "Fine, but keep that walkie-talkie on, and if all else fails then we meet each other at the car." They all agreed and exited the Suburban.

"Don't worry, Carmen," Jackson said. "You'll be safe with me." He nudged her with a friendly hip bump.

"Alright, let's do this then," Dominik agreed, as he lightly rubbed his hands together, rotating them in opposite directions as if forming a Play-Doh creation. They did a walkie-talkie check and split up heading down the two separate paths.

Pablo and Dominik began walking down the overgrown unkept path. Pablo went first and Dominik knew to just follow him but still be on the lookout. They may be saving the town, but Dominik still knew he had to keep Pablo safe.

"So, do you like my sister?" Pablo asked as they pushed through large overgrown branches. He didn't wait for a response.

"She definitely likes you. She trusts you or else she'd never let you help us. Or, actually, let you be alone with me."

"You know... I am just getting to know your sister and she's a great person," Dominik said. He was looking down at his feet bashfully kicking a few rocks out of the pathway.

"Oh, don't play cool, Romeo," Pablo said. "You took your dad's car to pick her up like some knight in shining car-mer. You probably dropped everything to do it, too. I'm sure you were watching some boxing match or something real machismo."

"That's a big overgeneralization, buddy. Plus, if you know that I like her, then why even ask?" Dominik shot back.

"Because your reaction is the fun part. I hope I'm not all secretive when I'm older," Pablo said.

They heard a few branches and leaves crunch loudly just behind them. They snapped into silence and looked at each other with eyes wide open. Dominik turned around, and Pablo got directly behind him. Dominik puffed his chest out, and Pablo felt safe. He didn't have an older brother but had a sense that this is what it would feel like if he did.

The sound shifted and went the opposite way.

"Okay," Dominik said. "It's probably just a bear or something."

"Oh yeah, a bear we can handle," Pablo said, trying to make light of the situation.

They continued walking along the path and began climbing up a small hill. The path once again split off into two different directions once they reached the top. Pablo inspected the area as every good detective should. "We need to go down the overgrown sloped path that looks more dangerous."

"How do you know?" Dominik said.

"See these branches here," Pablo said, pointing to the ground on the side of the path. "They were placed here. They aren't natural. This is the way. It's a clue," Pablo insisted.

"Alright, detective. Let's go then," Dominik said.

They made their way down the slope safely. The area opened with a small stream next to a gigantic thousand-year-old Doerner Fir. Pablo shined the light about 20 feet up the tree, and there lay a well-crafted tree house.

"Detective J. Do you copy? Over," Pablo said to Jackson via walkie-talkie.

Jackson and Carmen had been walking down the fire road with no other paths in sight. The moon was almost full and shined brightly on their path.

"Affirmative. What's your vector, Victor? Over," Jackson responded, holding the walkie-talkie directly over his mouth.

"Who is Victor?" Carmen asked.

"You have got to open your mind to other forms of entertainment. It's a joke from the movie *Airplane*. My grandpa loves watching it. We quote it all the time."

"I see," Carmen responded.

"We found the hideout," Pablo's voice rumbled through the walkie-talkie. "Make your way back to the correct path and turn right at the fake branches at the top of the hill. It leads you down a slope. The secret hideout is streamside. Over," Pablo said.

"10-4," Jackson responded. "See ya in ten. Over."

Carmen found the way they communicated amusing. It took her a moment to comprehend what they were saying to each other. It finally hit her, and she bobbed her head smirking.

"Of course, he was right," she said.

They turned around and walked toward the other path. It was about a mile away. Jackson saw a glimpse of light for a split second at the beginning of the path near the Suburban.

"We've been compromised. We have to hide," Jackson said, grabbing Carmen's arm and pulling her down to the ground. They were now crouching barely visible but still illuminated by the moon's gaze.

"What are you talking about?" Carmen whispered, surprised. She hadn't seen anything out of the ordinary.

"You looked down to fix your belt and missed the glimpse of light that seemed to be a headlight or flashlight. We must hide now," Jackson said pulling Carmen to the right side of the trail behind a large tree. They waited for a few minutes in silence, and a beam of light hit a tree across the way from them.

A voice yelled out loud enough to draw attention but in a creepy whisper. "I can smell you. We do get very hungry from time to time."

Carmen and Jackson covered their mouths. They crouched behind the tree and could tell that the person was standing on the road near them.

The walkie-talkie went off. "What's your ETA? Over." Jackson fumbled to silence the device, but it was too late.

"Fresh meat," yelled the figure in the middle of the road. How I've craved thee."

Carmen and Jackson stood up and ran deeper into the forest.

"Carmen! Follow me. I think we can still get there this way, but it won't be easy," Jackson said as he ran through the trees. Carmen trailed directly behind him.

The unknown figure saw their movement and began following them through the woods. "I will catch you," it said with an ominous chuckle at the end.

They jumped over logs and pushed through branches. The figure hadn't caught up with them yet, but they were still sprinting.

"There's a hill! Maybe it's the one that leads to the stream," Jackson said. They climbed to the top and saw the two paths directly in front of them. They stopped for a second to catch their breath.

"This is it," Jackson said. "Look where the branches are placed," Jackson said, pointing to the path on the left side.

"They look like normal branches to me. How do you guys come up with this stuff?" Carmen said.

Jackson scurried down the hill. Carmen followed directly behind him as cautiously as she could. They could hear someone still behind them.

"Pablo, over," Jackson said.

"Go ahead," Pablo responded.

"We have company. Prepare takedown upon entering the stream. Over," Jackson said.

"Roger," Pablo said.

Jackson and Carmen were now at the bottom and began to run along the stream. They could see the large tree in the distance. The unknown figure was still trailing behind them. As they whipped around the tree Dominik tackled the figure to the ground. He tried to hold it down, but the figure was too strong. They wrestled on the floor for a bit. Pablo had already made it up the tree and yelled to Carmen.

"Carmen, use this!" Pablo said as he threw down a large pickaxe. Its heavy steel head slammed into the ground, and Carmen ran over to retrieve it. The figure had thrown Dominik to the side and was headed directly for Carmen. She grabbed the pickaxe like a bat.

"Grand slam anyone!" Carmen yelled, driving the pickaxe directly into the dark figure's upper stomach. It immediately shattered into purple dust around her like an upset pimple.

"Direct hit," Jackson yelled.

Dominik scrambled to his feet, running to Carmen to see if she was okay. The dust cloud passed her by. She let her arms drop along her side with the pickaxe still in one hand.

"Six years of softball. It didn't stand a chance," she said, flipping her hair to the side. Dominik was staring at her in shock, a little turned on and a little freaked out.

"You guys have got to come up here!" Pablo said from the treehouse.

"How the heck did you get up there, monkey?" Carmen asked.

"A good detective never tells his secrets," Pablo responded.

He threw down a rope ladder and Jackson was the first to climb up.

"And here I thought I would need to protect you," Dominik said.

"I've been protecting myself since before I could remember. It would be nice to not do it alone though," Carmen said.

"Well hello, Carmen," Pablo said greeting his sister as she climbed into the tree house. "Get in before you are forced to crush another poor unfortunate soul," Pablo said.

"And he doesn't mean Dominik," Jackson added. They both laughed in unison. She stuck her tongue out at them in response.

"Woah, Swiss Family Robinson vibe," Carmen said as she looked around the tree house.

"Who?" Dominik asked upon entering.

"You're showing your dork side again, Carmen," Pablo said. "Remember guys don't like that."

"Uh, I do," Dominik interjected.

"Another love story, gross," Pablo said just before migrating his attention to the items in the treehouse.

"This is such an awesome spot. Frankie has thought of everything," Jackson said.

"It looks like he was preparing for an earthquake or something. Look at all this canned food. It's like a safehouse in here," Pablo said.

"Pablo, check this out!" Jackson said, staring at a large leather-bound book resting on a makeshift wooden table.

"Woah, this looks like it's from the 1800s or something."

"Trollipedia," Jackson read aloud.

"Such a cool name," Pablo said. "Why is it written in marker and duct-taped to the cover though? I think I have this same type of lined notebook paper in my school bag," Pablo chuckled.

"Maybe it didn't originally come with a name, so Frankie branded it," Jackson said.

"Yeah, that makes it even cooler," Pablo responded.

"This is fascinating," Jackson said as he opened it and flipped through the pages.

"It has all these other loose notebook papers in it. I bet Frankie added those also. Like holes in the mystery that he had discovered," Pablo said.

"Pablo, do you realize what we are holding?" Jackson asked.

"The answer," Pablo said.

"Precisely. The secret to what is going on and how we all can stop it," Jackson said.

The two sat down on the floor on what seemed to be a bed of sandbags. They had some research to do and buried their faces deep into the Trollipedia.

Carmen walked over to Dominik who was looking through a telescope.

"Find anything good?" Carmen said.

"Well, you're not on the other end so nothing that extraordinary," Dominik replied.

She began to blush.

"Smooth...So, would you say you wish you never met me?" She was usually so confident and carefree, but Dominik had a softening effect on her.

"My life would be so boring without you," he said. "I'd be scrubbing gum off the backside of the diner counter if I wasn't with you right now." They both chuckled.

"You called out sick from work for me?" Carmen asked.

"I told them I had a family emergency," he said as he looked into her eyes.

Usually, something so forward would scare her away. Her

mind would go to marriage and being tied down, left without her freedom and flirtations but with him it was different. This took her breath away because it was so honest. All she ever wanted was for someone to be there for her. She leaned in closer to him and they began to softly pucker their lips.

"Okay all, pow-wow!" Pablo said with his face still buried in the Trollipedia.

Carmen and Dominik backed away from each other in embarrassment and shuffled over to the boys. Carmen was relieved to see that the boys were not watching them and therefore didn't know about what would have been their first kiss.

"Hit 'em fact-ion Jack-tion," Pablo said, lifting his face up from the Trollipedia.

"It says that ghost trolls have been returning to the living world since cavemen roamed the earth," Jackson said.

"How did they get rid of them then? Did the dinosaurs eat them?" Pablo asked.

"Well, there was a big battle, but the cavemen managed to win it when they found the obsidian rock. I guess it has the power of extracting the ghost troll from the possessed human," Jackson said.

"Well, this just got all science-fictiony! Guess we aren't going anywhere without that rock," Pablo said.

Jackson continued reading to see if he could answer the next question that popped into his mind.

"Yup, obsidian rock and light shut the portal down. That's what Frankie was doing in that basement!" Jackson exclaimed.

"Rock and light. Nature's most precious items. We should have known," Pablo said.

"Wait guys, we are here too. Group discussion please," Carmen said.

"Alright, here is the short version for the basic people," Jackson said. "We are battling a troll species that was murdered by cavemen millions of years ago. They are now back for revenge using special ghosts that can travel through underworld portals to our world and possess us! Anyone could be a ghost troll."

"And they are trying to eat our babies and take over the world," Pablo added.

"Any questions?" Jackson asked.

Dominik was stunned and skeptical, his eyebrows now almost touching his hairline. Carmen's mouth lay half open waiting to speak but without the right words.

"Yes, question," Pablo said humorously, as if he were a planted actor in a studio audience. "How do we kill them and what if my dad is one of them? Can the troll ghost be extracted?" Pablo said in a high-pitched voice trying to impersonate a girl he once argued with in math class.

"Amazing question Ashleigh," Jackson said, playing along with Pablo's charades.

"Technically the ghost trolls can be killed by obsidian rock. This can happen when they are living in a human body or when they are in ghost troll form, such as our friend who turned to dust below. He was a ghost troll, so he died upon impact with the obsidian stone."

"Wait what?" Carmen asked. "So, there could be like, ghost troll people in this town already, and we still have to worry about the creepy flying purple people eating ones too?"

"That's what it says," Jackson replied. "The human features may be abnormally enlarged similar to that of a troll and over time morph into its own skin," explained Jackson.

"I bet you certain athletes are trolls already. Like, how are you seven feet tall, am I right?" Pablo joked.

Jackson nodded feverishly in agreement.

"Pablo, stop. So, Jackson, why is this barely happening now if they were killed so long ago? Carmen said.

"The Trollipedia says that the cavemen shut down the portals, but the town's founding fathers cracked them open in search of jewels. They began to realize an uptick in ghost presence, and the disappearance of children. They ultimately discovered obsidian stone and used it to defeat the ghost trolls. They sealed up the portals and created the Trollipedia. That's why this book is so old," Jackson explained.

"So, all that is missing is why Frankie?" Carmen asked.

"Frankie led us here to crack the case, so I say we continue forward," Pablo said.

"Well then, let's get that book into the right hands and get this all sorted out," Dominik said.

"Yes, but we have to shut down the next portal before more ghost trolls pass through it. It looks like we are almost out of time," Jackson said.

"Well then, let's grab some supplies and be on our way," said Dominik.

"Jackson look," Pablo said, hitting him on the shoulder. "These weapons all have black tips. It looks like the same rock from the necklace."

"Obsidian," they all said in unison.

"When I hit the troll with the pickaxe, he exploded," Carmen said. "These must be the weapons used to defeat them."

They began looking through the equipment and trying on different pieces. Pablo and Jackson both put on yellow hard hats with one light in the front, looked at each other, and did their secret handshake.

"Pew," they both whispered as their thumbs launched outwards like rockets.

Jackson grabbed one of the items from the floor and handed it to Dominik. "This one is for you. It's a mallet. Perfect for bashing evildoers over the head since you're so tall."

Dominik grabbed the mallet to feel its weight.

"It fits you and your black Suburban nicely," Carmen said.

Jackson picked up a smaller pick mattock and handed it to Carmen.

"We have already seen you in action with the larger one. Now, try this handheld one on for size. You can stick it right into your combat boot. It's called a pick mattock," Jackson said.

"Thank you," Carmen said with sincerity. "Fashionable and deadly."

The boys continued looking around and came across blue mining belts and shoulder harnesses. They helped each other put them over their yellow raincoats. They each had a pickaxe and shovel crisscrossed on their backs. Jackson's large backpack rested over his.

"Alright, now you guys look super cool," said Dominik, as he examined their troll-battling ensembles.

"Yeah, Pablo is just missing one thing," Carmen said.

"What?" Pablo asked. "This is perfect. What else could possibly be needed," Pablo said.

"Every good fighter needs a shield. You can place it right on your back just like Captain America," Carmen handed Pablo an old rusted circular gold mining pan. He looked unimpressed and didn't immediately reach for it. Jackson grasped the pan from Carmen and looked at it trying to see the vision.

"Yes!" Jackson exclaimed. "Look, Pablo, it even has straps already fastened. This must be what Frankie was thinking. We can learn to use all these weapons during different points of battle," Jackson explained.

"Oh, I see it now," Pablo said. "You did good sis…" He

patted her on the back and walked away slowly. "...this time," he said with a rebellious whisper.

Dominik looked over at their outfits in admiration. "Y'all look official. Like you're about to solve a crime, break some necks, and harvest some gold all at the same time."

"Wait, did you hear that?" Jackson asked. They all grew silent, staring at each other in fear.

Voices could be heard from outside the treehouse. Carmen ran over to the window.

"Uh oh, we got company! Two of them," she yelled. Pablo rushed to her side, and Jackson followed. "And boy are they ugly. So that's a man with a troll inside of him?" Carmen asked.

"Yup, troll humanoids," Jackson said. "Basically, the troll left the ghost form and became attached to a human. They are in a state of transformation."

"Yup! If they are really ugly, then they are still mutating with the human skin," Pablo said.

"They are fresh so hopefully weaker," Jackson added.

"Okay, so let's just call those types, trolls to make it easier," Carmen said.

"Get down here kids!" the troll yelled. "Or we will make you."

"Make us!" Pablo yelled, puffing out his chest.

The two trolls began to rustle around and were soon out of their sight. They all looked at each other and started to smell burning wood. Smoke filled the Treehouse.

"We need to get out!" Carmen yelled. "Now!"

Everyone began coughing and searching for a safe way out.

Jackson climbed on a box next to the window. "Pablo there's a rope or cord of some sort leading out of here. You think we can climb down it?"

"Or why don't we ride it?" Dominik asked, who had found a handlebar that was attached to it like a zip line.

"Genius!" Pablo exclaimed. "Frankie and I are spirit animals."

Carmen chuckled at Pablo's usage of the phrase "spirit animals". Even in a state of chaos, he brought her supreme joy. She usually would have corrected him but let it slide given the circumstances.

"Well, they do say great minds think alike," Jackson

responded.

"Jackson and Carmen, you guys go first," Pablo said. "You'll have to both hold on tight and slide right out of here."

"Are you sure, Pablo?" Carmen asked. "I don't want to leave you up here."

"I got him," Dominik interjected. He let out a soft smile and she nodded in agreement.

Carmen and Jackson climbed up to the window and grabbed the handlebars at opposite ends. Jackson fastened to the back of Carmen wrapping his legs around her.

"Here goes nothing!" Carmen said.

"Catch ya on the flip side, buds!" Jackson said, looking back at Pablo and Dominik just before pushing off from the window. The two flew through the shadowy night and in between large oak trees. The full moon shined bright on them as they soared through the sky.

Dominik and Pablo were up next. The flames began breaking through the floorboards.

"Time to go, little man," said Dominik in a rushed loud shout but Pablo was still on the other side of the treehouse searching for something. The flames roared, and Dominik could no longer see Pablo.

"Pablo! We need to go," Dominik yelled. "This thing is going to fall apart!" He couldn't see past the smoke but heard coughing in the far corner. He jumped through the growing flames to find Pablo collapsed in the corner.

"Oh no, you're not dying on my watch lil' buddy," Dominik said, throwing Pablo over his shoulder and making his way carefully back to the window. Pablo had passed out from the smoke but was still breathing.

"Let's hope this holds us both and that I don't drop you," Dominik muttered as he grasped the handlebars and kicked off from the window launching them into the night.

Pablo awakened as they glided through the cold crisp air. A nearby tree branch smacked him in the face. He coughed out the smoke in his lungs.

"Whoops!" Dominik cried out before letting out a sigh of relief. He wasn't certain that he'd wake up.

Pablo wasn't used to older male energy since his father was always so busy working. He embraced Dominik tightly so that he wouldn't fall off his shoulders. The smell of pine from the trees mixed nicely with Dominik's coconut and patchouli scent. Pablo thought to himself, two adventurers faced with death and saved by one another in the nick of time. He let out a smile and knew this was where he belonged. Berrymount was his home.

The zipline snapped from the burned treehouse side. Dominik and Pablo came crashing to the floor tumbling through the bushes right up to the heels of Carmen and Jackson.

"Well, don't you two know how to make an entrance," Carmen said.

Jackson realized Pablo was hurt and rushed over to him. "What happened?" Jackson asked. "Soldier down. I repeat soldier down. You were fine when we left."

Carmen grabbed Pablo in her arms. "Are you okay? Hurt? What happened?" Pablo was still coughing trying to catch his breath.

"He ran to look for something. Then the smoke got to him, and he passed out. I had to carry him out of there," Dominik said.

"You did?" Carmen asked, staring deeply at Dominik in awe of his bravery. Then snapped right back to Pablo. "What's wrong with you, monkey? Why did you do that?"

Pablo pulled the Trollipedia book from inside his pants belt region. "For this!"

"Woah, you got it! How could we have almost forgotten?

You're a genius," Jackson said. He grabbed the book and began looking through the pages while Pablo caught his breath. "It says right here that Dr. Reed's bookstore is the next portal. We have to get there fast to shut it down."

"Too late," Pablo said as he was looking over the town from the ridge. "There they go!" he shouted pointing up to the sky where six more ghost trolls launched into the night sky.

"These ghost troll things can't have every police officer under their spell," Dominik said. "I say, we go to the police station and get this thing sorted out."

"Well, I guess we can't argue with that, given the police station basement is actually the third portal," Jackson said.

"It's probably heavily guarded. It is a police station after all," Jackson added.

"It definitely makes the most sense," Carmen said. "We can't take these trolls on all by ourselves. We have the Trollipedia now, so maybe this is enough to show the police what we are up against. Hopefully, they can help."

"Let's head out troops. We've got a town to save," Dominik said.

"I could really use a cold Brisk right now," Pablo said as he struggled to stand.

"My favorite iced tea. Two please," Jackson added.

"Let's make that four," Dominik said, hip bumping Carmen. She smiled and bumped back flirtatiously.

The group walked back to the Suburban and headed for the police station.

Chapter 9: A Little Trickery

The police station was deserted. The lights were on inside, but there were no patrol cars out front. The wind blew leaves across the front steps and a chill ran across the entrance. They parked the Suburban directly in front of the entrance and made their way inside.

"Hello, anyone here?" Dominik said, pushing the large double doors open into the police station lobby. He looked around but there was no one in sight. The others followed behind him.

"Where is everyone?" Jackson asked.

"Maybe they went to a Halloween party," Pablo said, chuckling to himself.

"All the computers are still on though. It looks like they rushed out in a hurry," Jackson said.

"Must have been a party they just couldn't miss," Pablo said.

"Excuse me. Anyone here?" Carmen asked.

A head poked out from behind a cubicle. It was a short, very sinister, and almost serpent-like gentleman. He was smaller than average and wearing a tan suit with a white button-up. He stared at the group for a moment and then shuffled over silently.

"What seems to be the problem? Shouldn't you all be at the school?" he said, with his hands clasped behind his back as he slowly approached them.

"Sir," Dominik said. He cleared his throat. "We have reason to believe that the town is in danger and needs police assistance."

Carmen backed him up. "Yes sir," she said. "We would like to speak with the sheriff or whoever is in charge."

Pablo began retreating toward the door. He knew something wasn't right. Jackson turned to look back at him to see what was wrong and noticed the concerned expression on his face. He walked back slowly to meet Pablo shoulder to shoulder.

"I see," the man said.

"Why do these boys look like they are about to mine coal at church?" He stared deeply at the boys as if he knew more than he was leading on. Jackson and Pablo avoided his glare as if intercepting it meant they'd turn directly into trolls.

"He looks like a used car salesman," Pablo whispered to Jackson.

"And you're a black cat I take it. Interesting," the man said, now judgmentally focusing his attention on Carmen.

"This one obviously lacks creativity," he said with his eyes jumping to Dominik who was the only one not in a costume. He wore tan Timberland high-top boots with dark jeans and his football letterman's jacket. It had the letter "B" on the front. Dominik stared back at the gentleman eager to move the conversation forward.

"Sir, we'd be happy to explain. Can we go somewhere to speak?" Dominik made sure to show his respect and speak in a way that wouldn't get them into trouble.

"Why don't you just come back to the interrogation room then?" The man said as he opened the short swing door. He motioned them to walk into the station leaving the lobby area.

"Oh no, oh no," Pablo said, panicked. He now had everyone's attention. They stared directly at him waiting to hear what he'd say next. "Whoops," a concerned expression now covered his face.

"Pablo, stop. We are just going to tell him what's going on," Carmen said.

"I sharted," Pablo blurted out unexpectedly.

Dominik held in his laughter. His cheeks filled with air and his throat made a screeching sound. Carmen felt the same but was able to hold it in. She nudged Dominik to keep quiet out of respect for the officer. Her lips now held in the large smile that wanted to form.

"What did you say?" The man asked.

"I sharted. That's why I said, oh no, and I can feel it running down my leg. I need to use the restroom now," Pablo explained. He kicked the side of Jackson's foot.

"Oh, man! You stink! I can smell it. We better get you to the bathroom pronto," Jackson said to Pablo playing along.

Pablo grabbed his stomach and tensed up as if in bad pain. "Oww," he groaned.

"Sir, where is the nearest bathroom?" Jackson asked. "My friend has some bowel issues and I have his meds. If he doesn't get to the bathroom fast, he might crap all over the floor."

Pablo began to shake, "Oh no, I feel another one coming," he said. "A poop fart, an even bigger one. Where's the bathroom?"

Pablo started walking funny toward the officer. The officer stepped back dramatically, disgusted by Pablo.

"Yes, go! The bathroom is in the back," the man said. "You have five minutes. I will need to take you both into the interrogation room with the others."

The boys walked swiftly to the back and Pablo was walking stiffly as if holding something in. Jackson put his hands over Pablo's shoulder helping him along cautiously.

"I hope your brother is okay," Dominik said.

"Yeah, me too," Carmen said with a skeptical expression. She knew her brother well and this seemed suspicious.

"Come then. Let's go to the interrogation room, and you can share everything," the man said.

Pablo shut the door and stood against it so that no one would come in. He held his pointer finger to his lips.
   "Shhh," he whispered.

Jackson jumped gracefully doing a full 180. His arms flared around.

"I knew it," Jackson said. "You faker."

Pablo let out a moan. "Oh, my stomach," while Jackson made farting noises.

Dominik passed by the bathroom following the officer and turned back to Carmen. "Did you hear that? I think your brother really did crap his pants."

Carmen chuckled. The man led them into the interrogation room and closed the door.

"Okay, now get the Trollipedia out, Jackson. Let's find this portal," Pablo said.

The pair sat on the bathroom floor and navigated to the pages with the map of the police station.

"Hey, look," Pablo said. "There is a secret entrance to the portal through the file room if we move the bookshelf back."

"Let's do this. Silent but deadly," Jackson said. They poked their heads out of the bathroom door and crawled on the floor like spies. They had to pass the interrogation room and crawl under the window ever so quietly. Carmen, Dominik, and the man were still inside and did not seem to notice anything. They made it to the file room and began to close the door slowly but heard another door close at the same time. They stopped dead in their tracks. They heard the keys jiggle and assumed it was the man checking in on them.

The bathroom door creaked open, "Boys, are you okay in here?" The man said.

Jackson and Pablo knew this was their only shot. They closed the door gently and quietly began their investigation. There was only one bookshelf inside the room as the others were file cabinets. Pablo pointed to it and motioned his pointer finger in a circle to direct Jackson to look around it. They both began looking for a lever or some way to open it. They knew they only had so much time before the officer would try searching for them. Pablo knew he had to think like Frankie to open the bookshelf. This was in fact his secret entrance. He examined the books and found one slightly shorter than the rest. The title read, "Adventure in the Great Wide Somewhere," Pablo pulled on the book, and the bookshelf made a noise as if a latch had been lifted. Jackson and Pablo looked at each other with excitement. They pushed the bookshelf to the right with all their might. A cold draft blew into the room.

"It's pitch black in there," Jackson whispered.

Pablo motioned to their headlamps and they both turned on their lights. They started to realize exactly what the equipment was needed for as their missions progressed. They walked down the steep stairs and into the dark basement. A draft blew through it and the clanking of chains against the pipes startled Jackson. He jumped to the side of the wall as his heart skipped a beat.

"It's okay. Just the wind. What is this place?" Pablo asked.

"It looks like an old prison but for monsters or something," Jackson said. They walked past the open cells and saw chains fastened to the walls. The air was moist and steamy from the leaky pipes. Every once and a while, a water drop from above would hit various parts of their skin. Jackson flinched every time swiftly wiping the drop off. The wind moved through the metal cells and made whistling sounds. They walked slowly toward the back but felt lost.

"We need the map. We are wasting time," Jackson said. They stopped and pointed their helmets at the Trollipedia.

"Okay, it says we go left. Then it's at the far end with what appears to be drawings of the needed equipment," Jackson explained. They felt warmth on the back of their necks and could smell something foul.

"Pablo, did you shart again?" Jackson asked.

"Not it," Pablo joked.

"Actually, it's my breath," a voice said from behind them in a deep sadistic tone. The boys screamed and felt large clammy hairy purplish hands on both of their shoulders. They pushed and wiggled, but its grasp was too tight. The creature now held them both by their shirt collars high in the air. They were now once again face to face with a ghost troll, but this time they understood what it was. Jackson held on tight to the Trollipedia.

"Now, what do you think you are both doing here? No one should know about this place. Unless of course..." The ghost troll let out a deep hoarse breath before continuing. The boys cinched their faces together in disgust at the smell of its breath.

"You're here to halt our plans," the ghost troll said.

"What plans?" Jackson had seen enough action movies to know villains love to monologue.

"The destruction of your race of course," the ghost troll said. "We have arrived, and it's our time now. We must take back our land."

Jackson let out his deepest high-pitched scream which startled the ghost troll. Pablo pulled off the obsidian arrowhead necklace and held it high in the air.

"Not as long as we're here!" Pablo shouted as he slashed the ghost troll across the neck. It immediately dropped the boys and purple ooze began seeping from its neck. It grasped the wound with both hands, and the boys ran toward the portal.

"Hurry, left, left, left," Jackson screamed following behind Pablo. Jackson took the corner too quickly and his backpack snagged on a pipe valve. He tugged at it, but the backpack wouldn't budge.

"Pablo, help!" Jackson yelled out.

Pablo didn't realize Jackson wasn't directly behind him. He turned around swiftly and ran back.

"It's stuck. I can't break free," Jackson explained.

They both pulled at the backpack with urgency and just as the ghost troll turned the corner the backpack ripped, launching them backward to the ground. The Trollipedia fell out of Jackson's hands like a bad football fumble. The ghost troll bent down to grab it with one hand. Its other hand still holding its open neck wound. Pablo crawled over to the Trollipedia, and they wrestled with it in a tug-of-war fashion. Pablo managed to gain a tighter grip, and Jackson kicked the ghost troll directly in the forehead. The ghost troll lost its grip on the Trollipedia, and it slipped through its fingers but not before tearing a page out. The boys climbed to their feet. Jackson pulled the pickaxe from Pablo's back.

"Shall we trade?" Jackson said to Pablo.

Pablo grinned with joy passing the Trollipedia over and grasping the pickaxe firmly.

"I always wanted to play golf," he said as he positioned the pickaxe to the floor. He lifted it high in the air and yelled, "Four!" He swung the spike pick as hard as he could and made direct contact with the ghost troll's head turning him into a cloud of purple dust.

"Direct hit!" Jackson yelled out as he stood up waving the dust away from his face.

They looked at each other in utter disbelief and did their

secret handshake.

"Pew," they whispered at the end as their thumbs launched outward like rockets.

"Look there in the distance. It's glowing purple," Jackson said.

"It's portal time, my buddy," Pablo said.

They ran toward it and hoped they weren't too late. Everything looked to be in place to shut down the portal as if Frankie had already set it up. A wooden makeshift standing desk was nestled against the wall. It had all the necessary items as well as a generator for the spotlight.

"Let's set down the Trollipedia over there and figure out how to shut it down," Jackson said.

"Solid plan. You read, I'll move," Pablo said pointing to the desk.

Jackson opened the Trollipedia and flipped through the pages hoping that there might be a chapter called "How to shut down a portal."

"Found it! It looks like Frankie added in his own pages with new instructions," Jackson said.

Jackson began instructing Pablo on what to do. Pablo placed the nearby wooden stool directly in front of the portal that was now oozing purple slime. The large obsidian rock on the desk was about the size of a watermelon. Pablo lifted it with his whole body and placed it on the stool as Jackson described. Pablo then started the generator and adjusted the spotlight so that it was pointed directly at the rock and portal.

"It's working!" Jackson exclaimed. "The purple slime is drying out."

Pablo watched in amazement. "It looks like my week-old knee scab," he said.

Both boys were now equally perplexed and excited as they watched the portal harden completely. They stared as if it were a beautiful sunset falling into the ocean.

"It looks like elephant skin. Touch it," Jackson said.

Pablo walked up to place his hand on it. "It feels like Play-Doh," he said.

"Don't get stuck in it. You won't be able to get your hand out," Jackson said.

Pablo pulled his hand away quickly and the rock turned hard again.

They had successfully closed the portal before any more ghost trolls could enter. They celebrated with a happy dance and did their secret handshake.

"Pew," they both whispered as their thumbs launched outwards like rockets.

"Let's see if we need to do anything else with this portal before heading back," Jackson said.

"Smart thinking," Pablo said. They both collapsed to the floor for a moment of rest and began to look over the Trollipedia in more detail.

Carmen and Dominik were still locked in the interrogation room. The man never came back for them.

"I don't think he's coming back any time soon," Carmen said.

"It's okay. We will just wait then, and someone will come. Just tell the truth and see what happens."

Dominik grabbed Carmen's hand, and she felt a sense of comfort knowing he was so calm. She still knew deep inside that something was wrong though and that her little brother was probably up to something which is why the officer wasn't back yet. Had the man found them, she wondered.

"Jackson said the next portal was in the police station. I bet you they went to find it. We should have stayed with them," Carmen began beating herself up and assuming the worst.

"Hey, don't 'should' on us. We all decided. Let's see where it takes us," Dominik said, trying to ease Carmen's worries. She looked into his eyes, and he squeezed her hand three times as a sign of compassion.

"I didn't get to tell you before, but I like your black cat costume. You look really beautiful," Dominik said.

"Halloween is my favorite holiday. I love costumes that allow me to be in theme but still scratch skulls, ya know," Carmen replied with wit so she wouldn't blush and melt into his arms like heated caramel in light of a compliment.

"I'm all about functionality. Same reason I wore these boots," Dominik replied, tapping his Timberland boots together like Dorothy from *The Wizard of Oz.* The door began to rattle, and the man walked in startling the two.

"Well, it seems your little poop-filled detective friends are nowhere to be found," the man said. "Unfortunately, this is a very serious matter. Therefore, both of you must be put in jail until they are located. I will take one at a time. Young man, you first."

Carmen grabbed Dominik tightly. Her eyes told him not to

go. She didn't want to be alone there and knew something was wrong. He read her facial expression accurately but knew he shouldn't push back against the law.

"Wait, why don't you just leave us both in here then?" Carmen asked but the door shut before she could finish her sentence. She hoped Dominik would think of something. If not, then she'd have to make a run for it when it was her turn to be taken to the cell. She'd tackle the little man if she had to.

He followed the man out the door and walked slowly behind him grappling with what to do next. He knew being Black immediately made this whole situation riskier. His parents had taught him to stay away from the police at all costs. If he had to interact with them then sound as calm as possible, but this didn't feel right. These weren't ordinary police and the way this man was walking was almost animalistic. He knew he had to do something.

The man brought him to the cell door and opened it slowly. Dominik walked inside. He knew something was off but needed confirmation before acting recklessly.

"Wait," he said, grabbing the jail cell door. He was much stronger than the man, half his size.

"I have information that can help the trolls. Maybe if we all can just understand the larger problem, then an agreement can be made," Dominik said pausing for a reaction. The man's face went cold and his left eye twitched. "Without hostility," Dominik finished.

The man grew annoyed and said in a hissing type of manner, "The world will not be right again until you all are turned into slaves and your children are collected for troll consumption."

Dominik's face grew angry, and he lifted the officer by the collar with one hand. He held him in the air for a moment debating on what to do.

"Better we lock you up then," Dominik said, launching the man through the cell into the back corner. The man slammed against the wall and fell to the ground motionless.

"Definitely the wrong thing to tell a Black man shorty. Thanks for the confirmation. No more Mr. Nice Guy," Dominik said as he slammed the cell door.

The keys fell to the floor, and he picked them up to lock the stall. He knew now this was no joking matter. He had to step up and band together with the group to stop the trolls from total town domination.

Carmen was still sitting in the interrogation room staring at the wall in deep thought. Dominik rushed back unlocking the door. They locked eyes as he entered and smiled at each other. She ran into his arms.

"I knew you'd figure something out," she said, hugging him with a full-body embrace. Her face rested against his chest.

"This isn't a game anymore," Dominik said. They are coming for blood. We need to find the boys and get this mess stopped."

They held onto each other after the hug. Carmen looked into his eyes and felt as if she should kiss him. After all, he did save her life twice now.

The boys had made their way back up and closed the bookshelf passage. They opened the door quietly to see if anyone was around and poked their heads out. They could see Carmen and Dominik holding each other in the hallway.

"Get a room!" Pablo yelled. Dominik and Carmen pushed away from each other instantly.

"Now where have you guys been?" Carmen asked, shaking off the strong emotions she had for Dominik in this moment.

"Oh, you know, just saving the world. Thanks for distracting the creepy car salesman for us. Portal closed," Pablo said high-fiving Jackson.

"Alright all, let's do this. What's the next portal guys?" Dominik said as they walked out of the station and to the

Suburban.

"We aren't too sure of the details around the very next portal, but the school basement is after that," Jackson said.

"We had an encounter down there and this ghost troll beast ripped a page out," Pablo said.

"Yeah! Just before Pablo smashed him in the skull and into purple dust!" Jackson said all excited.

"Look at these little superheroes taking down trolls. I guess we head to the school then," Dominik said.

"Yeah, didn't the little troll dude say something about us needing to be there?" Carmen said.

"Guess we are going to find out," Dominik said.

Chapter 10: Back to School

The group was cruising comfortably in the Suburban toward the high school. They were still riding high on the success of closing the previous portal.

"Dominik, hit us with something relaxing to calm our nerves but still keep us amped," Pablo said.

"Oh, are you asking me to be the DJ?" Dominik said.

"That's exactly what I am asking. We got to see if you understand good music," Pablo said.

"My brother and I try to listen to a little bit of everything. I had this history teacher back in Los Angeles that did a whole lesson plan on music throughout the decades," Carmen explained.

"Yup, and she would show me all the songs. We'd discuss our favorites and rock out to the fun ones," Pablo said.

"Remember when I had you quiz me for the test by playing each song and making me name the artist and title?" Carmen asked.

"How could I forget," Pablo said. "It was the highlight of my life, until now."

"You guys must educate me. My grandpa only plays classical," Jackson chimed in.

"Well let's scan these channels and see if I can't hit you with the perfect song for this moment," Dominik said.

He hit the seek button on the radio but then remembered that his parents had all the classic rhythm and blues stations saved. He pushed number six on the saved stations.

"Try this one on for size my friends," Dominik said as he turned up the volume.

The unique sounds of "Smooth Operator," by Sade filled the air. Jackson and Pablo had their windows down and let their hands dance in the wind with the rhythm of the song. Carmen and Dominik noticed the two and looked at each other smiling in amusement.

They approached the High School slowly and noticed police cars, a packed parking lot, and all the lights on inside.

"Woah to the third power. This does not look safe. Danger D Robinson, danger. Drive past normally," Pablo said, now out of his seat and leaning on the center console in between Dominik and Carmen.

"Agreed. This is trouble," Jackson said from right next to

Pablo on the center console.

Dominik figured the boys knew what they were talking about at this point and decided to follow their advice. He drove at a normal speed and cruised past the front parking lot.

"There is a back parking lot just for the teachers up ahead. Let's go around there and see if we can scope out the place," Dominik said.

The teacher's parking lot, at the rear end of the school, was empty. The classrooms were all dark, and it felt eerie and desolate. It was completely opposite of the bright lights and cars on the other side.

"This all just seems too strange," Carmen said.

"You got that right, my sister," Pablo said. "We need to get down into that basement portal and shut it down before more come out. Jackson, check out the map to see where the correct spot might be."

"Looks like there is a secret tunnel in the ceramics room that gets us to the next portal," Jackson said with his head buried in between the pages of the Trollipedia.

"But Dominik, you are probably too big to enter," Jackson explained. "It looks like we will be walking alongside the pipes under the school."

"Star athletes just won't fit buddy," Pablo said patting Dominik on the back.

Dominik smirked and shot a glance at Carmen in the passenger seat from the corner of his eye. Beams of light began to dance around the inside walls of the school's rear entrance.

"Wait, wait, lights are coming from over there. Dominik, kill the engine," Carmen said.

Dominik quickly turned off the car and shut off his headlights. They all crouched down so as not to be seen but they were unfortunately the only car in the back parking lot. The doors to the rear entrance flew open, and two officers came through shining the lights out toward the parking lot. Everyone crouched down further in hopes of their car not drawing any attention. A flashlight hit the front windshield and the group let out a slight gasp.

One of the officers reached for his belt and grasped a walkie-talkie. "Sir, we got a suspicious vehicle out here. Were there any clearances put forth for a black Suburban in the rear parking lot? Over."

"No clearances were approved. All vehicles should be parked in front of the school. Over," said the voice on the other end in a strong direct manner.

"10-4," said the officer as he and the other one walked closer to the Suburban.

Carmen peaked her head up and saw the officers walking toward their car. She began to sweat and grew worrisome. They were about 100 feet away and approaching fast. Her brain began to construct a plan.

"What did you see? Are they walking toward us?" Dominik asked. He was starting to panic and sweat droplets began to form on his forehead.

"Yes, they are. Thinking. Thinking," said Carmen trying to come up with the best plan imaginable.

"Boys, duck down behind our seats and get as small as you possibly can. We'll recline the seats all the way back to hide you. When we leave, make your way into the school, and shut down that portal. You are both safer that way than getting locked up with these guys," Carmen said.

"Okay, sista," Pablo agreed. He looked toward Jackson, and they both nodded in unison.

Jackson and Pablo climbed to the floor and crouched into a ball-like position. Carmen and Dominik reclined their seats. Carmen stared deeply into Dominik's eyes as they both lay there silently. The moonlight bounced off her hazel eyes leaving them with a dark blue essence and directly into Dominik's heart.

"Do you trust me?" Carmen said.

"Sure, I do, but what's…" Dominik was cut off by the touch of Carmen's lips against his. Suddenly, he forgot about everything and melted into the seat. His body went limp for a moment. Then his hand reached up to meet her soft chin. Carmen had made the first move and kissed him. She too forgot about everything happening and grasped his shoulder pulling him closer.

"Um, what's that sound?" Pablo said as he heard their bodies moving against the leather seats.

Flashlights shined directly into both front windows.

"Hey, you kids, what do you think you're doing in there?" The officer on the driver's side tapped his flashlight on the window.

Carmen and Dominik were so engrossed in each other that they could barely hear the outside world.

The other officer on the passenger side began to tap the window as well. "This is unacceptable, and everyone should be inside the High School. We are on a city-wide curfew!" he yelled.

Carmen pulled away from the kiss, and Dominik was motionless. His eyes were still shut, and his lips pierced frozen in time.

"Alright, you love birds! Break it up. We know this is just so magical for you both but time to cut it out," said the other officer banging on Dominik's window once again.

Dominik snapped out of it and opened the door first. He climbed out of the car calmly. The officer grabbed his arm firmly, motioning him to stand directly in front of him. Dominik followed his direction. Carmen opened the car door as well, and the officer motioned his hands toward the school.

"Sorry, sir," Carmen said. "We didn't know."

"Yes, sorry about this officer," Dominik added.

"Now you kids can't be out here. This town is under lockdown. It's not safe. We'll accompany you to the gymnasium with the other teenagers. All your parents are being briefed in the theater," the officer said.

"Yes, sir," Dominik and Carmen said together. They stayed quiet and began walking toward the school. The officers stayed close behind them.

Jackson and Pablo were still nestled in the back seat of the Suburban behind the reclined chairs.

"Is the coast clear?" Jackson said to Pablo after a few

minutes.

"Let me inspect the situation," Pablo said while climbing out from the small space behind the reclined seat and poking his head out silently to see over the dash. "All clear. Time for some real trouble."

"Good, because I'm getting a cramp in my right leg. Can you imagine if you were a magician's assistant and you always had to hide in weird positions during magic tricks?" Jackson asked.

"You know, I would really hate that," Pablo said. "It's like, how does the woman pull her legs up into that box when they are doing the sawing trick?"

"She must be double-jointed or something," Jackson said as he readjusted his socks and pant legs.

"Or maybe she doesn't have any legs," Pablo responded. He stared blankly into space looking for a viable answer.

"Touché," Jackson said. He packed up his bag, and they both readjusted their gear. The two slithered out of the car slowly like cobras on the hunt and closed the car doors quietly. They made their way toward the back of the Suburban and crouched down. They were in their most stealthy ninja pose.

"Okay, plan of action," Pablo said.

"Yes, a thought, let's enter through the science lab window and make our way into the ceramics room which is just across the hall. Then take the tunnel in the storage closet to the portal," Jackson said as he had already mapped out the route while he was looking at the Trollipedia.

"How do you know where everything is?" Pablo was surprised by all his knowledge of high school.

"My grandpa loves pottery. He substitute teaches for the ceramics class sometimes and I got to visit him there...Twice. I loved it so much that I paid attention to every detail," Jackson explained.

"Your grandpa is so cool," Pablo replied. Jackson shook his head in full agreement. "Follow me, soldier. Silence mode from here on out. Military hand signals only."

Pablo made his way around the driver's side of the Suburban still crouching in classic ninja form. They scurried undetected like raccoons hunting for trash cans in the dead of night. They went from the car to the bushes bordering the school and dove through them like well-trained circus acrobats one after the other. They were now directly next to the school's wall and out of sight thanks to the large bushes. Pablo motioned with his hands pointing two fingers at Jackson and then switching directions with another point.

Jackson moved past Pablo and made his way along the wall

to the science lab window which was slightly open. Unfortunately, many science projects went wrong in that classroom, so they had to frequently air out the room in the evenings. The window was usually always slightly open. Berrymount was a safe town, so break-ins or theft were never really a big concern.

Jackson used his two pointer fingers and motioned as if he was going to enter through the window. Pablo nodded his head in confirmation with a serious grin and planted himself firmly on the ground on his hands and knees. Jackson stepped on Pablo's back, using him as a human stool to enter the classroom window. He launched his body through the open window and landed somewhat gracefully on the other side. He climbed to his knees dusting himself off. Once he knew the coast was clear, he put a thumbs-up hand gesture out the window. He searched around the room for something Pablo could step on so that he too could enter through the window. Jackson made it to the teacher's desk and found a sturdy tin trash can. He took a deep breath and held it in while carefully taking the dirty trash bag out of the can. Apparently, the science teacher had previously thrown away remnants of leftover tuna casserole. Jackson dropped the bag in the nearby sink and let out his breath. He went to the window, dropping the trash can down to Pablo. Pablo placed it steadily on the floor. grabbed Jackson's hand that was reaching out the window and climbed inside.

"Successful entrance of the perimeter," Pablo said now safely inside the classroom. "Hopefully, Frankie set everything up already at the portal so that it's easy in and out. Maximum ghost troll annihilation."

"Do you think any ghosts will be guarding the portal like last time?" Jackson asked.

"I sure hope not. It's spooky enough just being in this high school," Pablo replied.

"I can't wait until I get to high school," Jackson said.

"A Billy Madison movie quote! This is why we are best friends," Pablo said.

"Let's move. It smells funky in here," Pablo replied as they both made their way to the exit door of the science lab. Jackson let out a slight chuckle. "Freakin' tuna casserole."

Jackson pulled open the door a bit, and it made a loud creaking sound that startled Pablo. They looked at each other in fear. Jackson let out a deep breath and slowly pulled the door fully open.

Pablo poked his head outside the door and the hallway was completely dark. He motioned for Jackson to cross the hallway into the ceramics classroom. Both classroom doors faced each other. Jackson laid flat on his stomach and crawled in military form across the hallway while Pablo kept watch. Jackson reached up to open the ceramics classroom door and the wind from the open science lab window spiraled through the hallway flinging the ceramics classroom door wide open. It banged against the wall making a large crash that echoed through the vacant halls. Jackson looked back at Pablo and their faces were both in utter shock. Jackson scurried into the ceramics classroom to hold the door still so that it wouldn't bang once again.

The school loudspeaker went off startling the boys.

"Students and faculty, please remain calm. The police are doing what they must at this time. We will return shortly with any updates. Thank you," said a voice that sounded like a 1980s robot.

Jackson motioned Pablo to crawl over. As Pablo left the science lab doorway crawling on his stomach, the wind blew the door shut. It slammed loudly. The two boys locked eyes, and Jackson began waving his hands for Pablo to hurry. Pablo crawled swiftly to the door but was stopped in his tracks when the corridor doors opened. A voice came from a radio of some sort. Jackson grabbed Pablo's hands and pulled him in.

"Return with status on the south corridor. Unknown noises heard, over," the radio sounds echoed through the empty halls.

"10-4, walking that way now. Over," said the officer who was walking down the hallway. He was due to pass Pablo and Jackson any minute. They began to quietly shut the ceramics classroom door. The officer peered into each classroom window to see if he could see anything. He was now in between the computer lab and ceramics doors and noticed the feeling of cooler air. He turned to face the ceramics class and shined his flashlight through the door window as he approached. The boys hid behind the door and watched as the light flashed onto different objects in front of them. The officer grasped the door handle, and it shook a bit inside the room above the boys' heads. They scurried away from the door just in case the officer opened it.

A noise came from the science lab room just before the officer could turn the handle. He swiftly changed directions and opened the science lab door. He felt the cool breeze and walked into the room with his flashlight. He noticed the wind blowing the blinds and the sound of them rattling. Just then the door slammed shut once again letting out a loud bang. The officer let out a light scream like a frightened child. The boys, still hiding in the ceramics room, jumped with fright as well but then began to chuckle, covering their mouths as they heard the officer scream with fear.

The officer walked over to the window. "Darn wind," he said as he slammed it shut. "False alarm, over. Just the wind playing tricks on us." He opened the door and shut it behind him then walked back down the hall and out of sight.

"That was a close one," Jackson said.

"Sure was. Let's move forward," Pablo said.

The ceramics classroom was dark and scary. It smelt of clay and the moonlight barely shined through the open skylight. They managed to find the closet and along both walls were the completed ceramics from the high school students. Mugs, themed jewelry boxes, vases, and bowls were all in different sizes with interesting colors. They closed the closet door behind them and turned on their mining helmet lights.

"Woah, these high schoolers are really creative. Look at this tall coffee mug with a pirate face," Pablo said. "Argh Jackson, you must drink me."

Jackson smirked at Pablo's joke. He began looking at the ceramic pieces also. He found a large misshapen bowl and held it up.

"This thing is the size of my head. What the heck is it supposed to be?" Jackson asked.

"Some type of wannabe salad bowl," Pablo said. "The kid who made that definitely got an F on it. Why is it puke green?"

"Poor color choice for sure. We need to take this class when we get to high school," Jackson said.

"It's a must-do for the holiday season. That way we can just make our loved ones Christmas gifts and not have to buy anything," Pablo explained.

"Hey! That's what this person did. Look at this weird Christmas-themed jewelry box. It's got a tree, snowman, presents, and everything," Jackson said.

"I bet it's for his mom," Pablo said inspecting it. "Hideous but thoughtful. I think the thought counts here."

"Ditto. Now the map said the tunnel should be in the deep right corner behind a shelf," said Jackson.

They went to the right corner and could see that this shelf did not have ceramics on it but piles of books. They went on both sides of the shelf and began to tug and pull in hopes of moving it. It took all their might to slide the shelf over to the right side and behind it was a cube-shaped air vent wide enough for two short-bodied individuals.

"Well, we were right. Dominik is way too big to fit in there," Jackson said.

"Yeah, this is for the shorties," Pablo said. "Shoot, you might outgrow this tunnel by the time we get to the nineth grade."

"My height is a blessing and a curse. I really don't want to be even more lanky than I already am," Jackson said.

"At least you won't get picked last in sports," Pablo said.

"Hey, you could be the star basketball player and I'll be the stumpy charismatic mascot!"

"Now that sounds fun," Jackson said.

They got down on their hands and knees and began to crawl through the vent. It was fairly clean inside, so they knew Frankie had been through here recently. They shuffled their bodies for about 12 feet until approaching a big drop-off. It had a rope fastened to the ceiling.

"Well, looks like that's the end of the road. We are going to have to climb down this rope. Hope you did well in gym class climbing," Pablo said.

"Guess I'm conquering my fear of heights today," Jackson said.

Pablo grabbed hold of the rope, and it felt steady. He knew Frankie put it there so the fear that it would come undone or break as soon as he took hold was non-existent. He trusted Frankie even though he never actually knew him. He felt like they were kindred spirits. He slowly climbed down the rope and got to the bottom in about 30 seconds. It was about a 15-foot distance.

He called up to Jackson, "It's not even that far. Michael Jordan-size you know."

"Looks like giraffe size to me, but okay," Jackson said as he grabbed the rope and shimmied down. He still reached the floor in record time.

"You're a pro. High five!" Pablo said to Jackson in a whisper. Their hands smacked each other gently. They were both now securely on the floor in what seemed to be some type of plumbing and electrical space beneath the school.

It was fairly dark except for some overhead lights flickering here and there. Luckily, they had their mining helmet lights on and pointed them around the area to see what lay ahead of them.

"Better get your pickaxe ready. Who knows what we will find down here," Pablo advised Jackson. They walked slowly through the walkway, which had a concrete wall on the right and big pipes all along the left side.

"Map said to continue down this path until we get to a dead end. Then we go right, and it should open up a bit just before hitting the portal," Jackson explained.

"Much appreciated, navigator," Pablo said.

They followed the paths and the pipes leaked water all over the floor.

"Is this place even sanitary? Smells like teenager farts,"

Jackson said.

"Carmen's friends probably come down here to let out steam before going to their next class," Pablo joked.

"They call this the Fart-ment," Jackson said. They both chuckled.

"Yeah, and then all the students hold their farts in during class and let them out only in here so that it adds to the stench," Pablo added as they laughed quietly.

A loud bang came from one of the pipes that they had passed a minute ago. Pablo looked back at Jackson in fear. They stopped dead in their tracks and listened for a moment more. Nothing else could be heard besides the leaking of water and wind blowing through the hallway. They began to move faster.

"You'd think the ghost trolls would be down here guarding it, making sure it isn't shut down. The police station portal had a guard," Pablo said.

"They must not be that smart. Or maybe they haven't been on Earth long enough to figure out all the portals," Jackson said.

"Well, that sinister looking one at the police station seemed to have been here forever and he wasn't big like the other troll humans. He looked more like the Penguin from that one Batman movie," Pablo said.

"Please don't bring up that movie at a time like this," Jackson said. "My uncle was watching it and I thought it would be fun but instead, got nightmares."

"My bad. I totally understand," Pablo said. "The other Batman movie with the Joker still haunts my dreams."

"It's that creepy dance he does," Jackson said.

"Exactly! I hope to never hear that 'Partyman' Prince song again," Pablo said.

"Ha, you even know the name of it," Jackson gasped.

"Okay, subject change," Pablo said. He started to become more fearful of their current scenario the more they discussed movie villains.

"The Trollipedia said some trolls may still be in the town and are unknown to Frankie which is why it says to trust no one," Jackson said.

"I sure hope there aren't more secret troll agents. Hey, I see an opening," Pablo said.

They were now at the end of the walkway, and it opened into a larger area. The portal lay in the back corner glowing purple and slimy as it prepared itself for opening. They could see the workstation for Frankie nestled in the corner. He had all his supplies laid out and the light set was there with a generator. He even had the desk lamp light still on.

"This was Frankie's desk. All his supplies are here. He was planning to come back here tonight," Jackson said.

Jackson and Pablo had moved a few things around on the desk, and at the very bottom lay a map of the school. It had certain places circled with writing above it. The lunchroom said "mean," three of the classrooms had big Xs over them, and one area was circled which seemed to be an outdoor seating area.

"Hey, maybe the circled one was his favorite place," Pablo said optimistically, trying to focus on the positives of the map.

"I don't think Frankie had many friends. He seemed to be a bit lonely," Jackson said as they assessed the map deeper.

"He *seems* lonely. Present tense. He isn't truly gone yet," Pablo said.

"Well, he did get pulled into the underworld. It's unlikely someone would come back from that."

"But these ghost trolls are doing it, coming back, maybe he can too," Pablo said, just hoping for the best.

"True," Jackson said sincerely after deeply thinking about

that option. "He does know the species."

"What if we tried to find him," Pablo said. "Enter the portal and free him."

"Two kids going into the Underworld is definitely a low probability of survival," Jackson said. "He would really like us though...I think."

"Yeah!" Pablo exclaimed. "And we could form our own portal guarding crew. The whole town would treat us like royalty because we saved them. He'd be the coolest kid in town! Our Frankie San, like a sensei!"

"True," Jackson agreed." "And then he wouldn't be made fun of or have to hide out alone in a dirty basement... A boy can dream," Jackson said with respect.

"Let's make a pact then. In the future, we go into the portal and bring him back," Pablo said with all seriousness.

"We'd have to do a proper assessment to make sure we can get back home and that nothing would eat us," Jackson said.

"Of course. All the right precautions," Pablo confirmed.

They grew silent, both trying to think about how that could happen. It seemed like a nice thought, but they were barely getting through their current situation and didn't even know if they'd make it out alive or to the 7th grade in one piece. They both rummaged around the area some more and prepared the equipment. The portal would open soon.

Jackson found an old photograph of a man and a woman posing in front of the ocean. It seemed to have fallen to the floor as they were moving things.

"Pablo, look at this," Jackson said, holding the picture up.

"Wow, it's probably Frankie's parents. His mom is so pretty. Do you think she is wondering where he is? Pablo asked.

"His story is a sad one actually. He lost his dad and mom. He lives above Berdaldo's Grocery store, alone," Jackson replied.

Pablo's face grew gloomy, and he almost fell into tears. The portal began to rumble, and the bright purple coloring started to expand slowly across the rock.

"It has begun. Can't cry now. Cry later. Let's do this," Pablo said.

"For Frankie," Jackson replied with his fist out signaling Pablo to complete their secret handshake.

"Pew," they whispered at the end as their thumbs launched outward like rockets.

Jackson turned on the tall light fixture, grasping it with two hands. Pablo saw the stool in place directly in front of the portal and carried the large obsidian rock over from the tool bench area. The light hit the stone, reflected a bright green beam onto the portal. Pablo moved the stone closer to the portal in the hope that it would speed up the process, but a giant purple troll ghost hand came out of the portal flailing wildly. It knocked the stone from the bench to the floor. Pablo dropped to his knees to immediately pick up the bench and rock for repositioning, but the giant arm was still flailing looking for something to grab. He tried to stay out of its grasp but now that the portal wasn't being shut, the second arm of the ghost troll pushed through the portal as well. Jackson remembered the shovel on his back but had trouble grasping it. Pablo set up the stool but lost his footing while picking up the rock. The large hairy purple ghost troll's arms wrapped around Pablo's neck, placing him in a chokehold.

"Jackson!" Pablo yelled out.

Jackson finally pulled the shovel from his back and struck the ghost troll's arms trying not to hit Pablo. Jackson's blows with the shovel were not phasing the ghost troll. Its cantaloupe-sized head came through the portal forehead first. It was somewhat transparent but still sweaty and sticky with purple slime. Jackson knew his strength was no match for the ghost troll. He scanned the room for another solution. He looked at the shovel's head and noticed the pointy part at the end was black. He grasped the shovel over his head, and with all his might jammed it directly into the ghost troll's forehead. It let out a high roar and its head began to disintegrate into purple dust as its fate gradually made its way to the arms choking Pablo. Pablo fell to the ground, free from its grasp. Jackson grabbed the light, and Pablo lifted the stone onto the stool. They finished sealing off the portal, together. It hardened into rock once more and the boys collapsed to the floor exhausted.

"We are getting really good at this," Pablo said out of breath touching his neck where the ghost troll had choked him.

"Professional ghost troll guards," Jackson replied.

"Or just simply, **The Ghost Guard**. We wouldn't want to scare people too badly with the whole troll story," Pablo replied.

"Yeah, you're right. A ghost alone is scary enough. Too complicated for the weak-minded," Jackson added.

"Frankie would be proud. Plus, his father was in the Coast Guard," Jackson said.

"Oh yeah," Pablo said. "He was in a uniform in the picture we found.

They both held a moment of silence and saluted each other in solidarity. They packed up and began their journey the same way they came.

Jackson led them through the pipes, up the rope, and back into the ceramics closet. They put the bookcase back as it was and opened the closet door quietly. Unfortunately for them, a police officer was standing in the classroom entrance doorway with his back facing them. Jackson rushed to shut the door, and a gust of wind pushed on him causing the door to slam shut.

"Jackson!" Pablo whispered intensely.

"There is someone out there. Should we fight him?" Jackson said with his body pressed against the door.

The door opened and pushed forward a bit. "Who is in there?" The officer said.

Pablo ran to the door to help Jackson push it closed, and it slammed shut once again. The officer got on his radio and began to speak. The boys could barely hear what he was saying.

"He's calling for backup. I just know it," Jackson said. The door began to rattle, and the boys tried to keep it closed using all their body weight.

"We are caught, Pablo. If we don't surrender, they will find the portal entrance," Jackson whispered.

"Shoot, you're right. Mission blown," Pablo responded.

The two officers were now at the door pushing it open. The boys looked at each other and let go at the same time fleeing to take cover, but Jackson fell to the floor. The officers launched into the room.

"Do you guys know where the bathroom is?" Jackson asked still lying on the floor. He tried to act cute and innocent with his body squeezing inward like a puppy after being scolded.

The officer looked at him and said, "You should be with the other kids. How did you get over here?"

Jackson froze for a couple of seconds without responding. Pablo jumped out from his hiding place and stood beside Jackson.

"He was looking for me, officer. I get diarrhea sometimes really bad, and it's embarrassing going to the bathroom with all the other kids because they hear you farting and then start rumors about you, so I tried to find the furthest bathroom, but then got scared and hid, crying, alone and sad."

The officer looked completely puzzled and was at a loss for words. Pablo went on.

"One time, Georgie St. Petersburg III took a fat dump during lunch in the main bathroom, and he got called 'Dump Truck' for the rest of the school year. I just couldn't be subjected to that type of ridicule right now with losing my mom and my sister being into only loser guys who…"

"Okay, okay, we get it," the officer said. Pablo's babbling began to annoy him. "You should be back in the cafeteria with the others though. We believe you know the way back."

Pablo and Jackson began to walk, and luckily Jackson had known the layout, or else they'd be completely lost.

The other officer was staring at Jackson and Pablo walking directly in front of him.

"So, what are your Halloween costumes supposed to be anyway? I don't understand the reference."

"Don't all men share the same fascination with gold and crime?" Pablo asked, standing tall with his chin held high. He was trying to be macho like his *papá*, Martin.

The officer nodded in agreement and the other officer said, "Kid, why do you think we are cops?"

Jackson and Pablo didn't understand the joke, but fake laughed with the officers.

"The problem is those axes and shovels could be used as weapons. We will have to confiscate them," the first officer said.

The boys began reaching for their shovels and pickaxes,

handing them over to the officers.

"Excuse me sir, but why are the kids being quarantined in the cafeteria?" Jackson asked while the officers fumbled with their mining gear.

"There is some terrorist activity going on in town so we have locked down everything until we can locate the root cause. Everyone is a suspect at this point," the first officer said.

The boys looked at each other and Pablo mouthed, "Terrorist" in a surprised manner. His right eyebrow raised, and his face scrunched up as he said it.

"So, this is for our safety then?" Pablo asked the officers.

"Yes, your safety is our top priority," the officer responded.

"These guys are the real cops then," Pablo whispered to Jackson.

"Yeah, I can tell. Plus, I have seen them around town," Jackson responded.

"Thank you for your service gentleman," Pablo said to the officers.

"You're welcome, son," one of the officers responded.

CHAPTER 11: An Uproar in the Cafeteria

The officers opened the cafeteria doors and the boys walked into a sea of at least two hundred elementary and middle school kids. Given that it was Halloween night, everyone was dressed up in their favorite costumes. Many of them were huddled in groups talking and seemed to be enjoying the time with their friends. A few of the princesses and ballerinas could be seen braiding each other's hair. The superhero crew was playing the slap hand game, and let's not forget the countless lions, tigers, and bears running around aimlessly causing a ruckus.

Jackson and Pablo located a spot up against the wall with the least number of kids around so that they could discuss their next move. They sat cross-legged in front of each other.

"Okay, first off, why are there only kids in here?" Pablo asked. "I don't see any of the high schoolers."

"Yeah, it's basically elementary and junior high here. There must be a reason for it," Jackson replied.

"Maybe teenagers are just harder to handle so they keep them separate," Pablo said. "I can't get Carmen to do anything she doesn't want to do."

"Or the trolls hunt them down first, just for sport," Jackson said. "Then they save the kids for later."

"Twisted but a definite probability," Pablo replied.

"Hey, did you guys come from the outside? What's going on out there?" said a girl about their age as she sat down cross-legged. Her black Dr. Martens with purple roses on the side slammed into the floor beside them.

She looked to be an outsider type as well. She was dressed in a punk rocker costume, but it almost seemed like elements of it were a part of her daily wardrobe. Her jet-black hair was styled in a femme faux afro with purple tips. She had on an oversized white T-shirt with an image of a black skull in a purple mohawk splattered across the chest. Her pants were equally exciting given they were plaid but two different colors on each pant leg, mustard yellow and crimson red. She wore a black leather jacket that seemed to belong to someone much older than her beforehand. Her eyes had purple makeup around them which shot outward toward her ears like flames from a rocket launching into orbit. Large silver hoop earrings, a black choker, multi-colored bangles, and fingerless gloves completed her ensemble.

Jackson was immediately impressed. Such authentic commitment to the holiday accompanied by a fearless attitude he thought. He stared at her in awe as she spoke and finally took a breath when she finished speaking. They all sat in silence for a few seconds.

"Should we tell her?" Jackson turned to Pablo, breaking the awkwardness.

"Classified information," Pablo said, whispering only to Jackson and speaking out the right side of his mouth. He had no interest in including this girl in their conversation. He pretended like she wasn't there.

"I can still understand you both," the girl said. She turned to Jackson ignoring Pablo.

"Well, they told us there is some type of terrorist attack happening and we all need to stay inside. But I'm like, why can't I be with my parents?" she explained.

"Classic totalitarian take-over method," Jackson said.

"Yeah, exactly," the girl said. "This is real fishy. Plus, not everyone is at school. What about those people in their houses? How are they patrolling them and making sure they aren't the culprits? They have some of the teenagers in the gym and the parents are in the theater listening to the sheriff and principal speak," she explained as if they had asked her what she knew.

"How do you know all this?" Pablo asked.

"I am just very aware of my surroundings, and I watch people," the girl said. "My mom can never keep a secret from me because one way or another I'll find out exactly what's really going on."

"Just like a detective," Jackson said.

"I guess so," she said. "Are you guys dressed as detectives? What's with the hard hat? And what's that necklace made of?"

She grabbed at the obsidian arrowhead necklace around Pablo's neck that he was fidgeting with, and he pulled away instantly.

She realized that she had made him uncomfortable so continued rambling, "Never mind it. I like unique things. As you can see, I'm a bit hardcore," she said, leaning back a bit to show off her full ensemble. Her right hand lifted, making an upside-down half-moon shape to emphasize her full outfit.

"The punk rock outfit is really cool," Jackson said, making a horns sign with both hands. She smiled at his natural dorkiness.

"So, what's your name?" Jackson asked.

"Jenelle. I've seen you around," she said to Jackson. "But don't really know him," pointing her thumb at Pablo.

"Uh, the him has a name and I'm with Jackson all the time..." Pablo responded.

"Okay, but it doesn't mean that I've seen you before," Jenelle shot back.

"Well, you are kind of new here," Jackson said to Pablo, agreeing with her.

Pablo shot Jackson an annoyed expression as he felt like he was taking her side.

"Anyways..." Pablo said to Jenelle with a fake smile. "We ought to get back to our mission now. Could you excuse us?"

Jenelle rolled her eyes at Pablo. The cafeteria door opened, and two police officers walked in with the principal. Pablo, Jackson, and Jenelle immediately halted their conversation and watched as the officers and principal made their way to the stage in the back of the cafeteria.

Pablo lightly elbowed Jackson on the arm. "Be on the lookout," he mouthed.

Jackson nodded with seriousness and Jenelle saw their interaction from the corner of her eye.

The principal now stood center stage with a microphone in front of him and two officers on either side of him.

"Hello, kids," he said. "I know you all are eager for an update. Your parents have been briefed on what is going on and everyone should be able to return to their homes in the next few hours," he continued. "There was a terrorist threat to our town, but we believe everyone will be safe. We just need more time for further investigation. Your parents are in the theater with other loved ones. Please continue to stay calm and we will be back momentarily with another update. We will leave Officer Rosas here for your safety."

The principal and other officer left the stage, and all the kids began to whisper and blurt out questions.

"Any casualties, sir?" spouted off an obvious class clown. Everyone snickered.

"When can I see my mom?" said a girl in the crowd.

"What's for dinner!?" another one shouted as some kids chuckled.

There was an equal amount of uneasiness and excitement in the room. Kids began playing tag and bumping into each other as others sat in groups discussing what could be going on. The principal and officer exited the cafeteria while Officer Rosas stood on stage with his hands clasped behind his back in a military-style stance. A few girls approached the bottom of the stage hurling questions at him, but he stood in silence.

Pablo leaned over to Jackson. "That officer appears to be larger than usual, don't you think?" Pablo asked.

"Yeah, and uglier. He is much bigger than a lot of people in this town. The principal used to be shorter too and now he looks like a giant cockroach," Jackson said.

Jenelle poked her head into their huddle and spoke.

"Mr. Rosas knows my daddy and I've been to a few of his backyard barbecues. Looks like he's been hitting the gym and carne asada a little too hard if you ask me. What are you guys getting at?"

"Or he's one of them," Pablo said.

"One of what?" Jenelle looked confused.

"Precisely," Jackson said, agreeing with Pablo.

Jackson and Pablo began playing ideas out in their heads silently. Their eyes moved ever so slightly as if they were jumping from side to side.

"Jackson...and Jenelle," Pablo said. "This is our moment. We have got to show the others what's going on. Everyone is in danger. We need a plan."

"I'm in," Jenelle said, eagerly slapping her hands together just as Pablo finished the last syllable in his sentence. She was bouncing back and forth with her hands pressed tightly together, one hand making a fist and the other grasping it.

Jenelle was the type of person who was up for any adventure. She had three brothers, but they were all much older than her. She had always wished that she could have grown up with them. They'd tell exciting stories of conquering haters, climbing trees, and football with Dad. She hadn't been born yet and always felt like she missed out. Her parents were a bit older now and less spontaneous. They owned their own cajun creole barbeque joint outside of town so most of her time was spent helping them or tending to her grandma while they were working. She was always so busy and had little time to build friendships. She naturally yearned to be a part of something bigger.

"Don't you want to make sure you're okay with the plan first?" Jackson asked.

"I trust you guys," Jenelle responded with confidence as she put her hand out in the middle of them. "Let's save the world."

"That's the spirit!" Pablo exclaimed, placing his hand over hers. He had his doubts about her before, but anyone who could laugh in the face of danger was a friend in his eyes. Plus, he could tell Jackson liked her.

"Let's pull the troll out of him in front of everyone. This will get the kids on our side so we can break out and shut down the last portal," Jackson said.

"Wait, like a real troll?" Jenelle said surprised but still up for the challenge. She wanted to also ask about the portal but didn't want to seem out of the loop.

"Yup. I just need to look over the Trollipedia one more time," Jackson said, and he fished the book out of his backpack. He laid it on the floor and began flipping through the pages.

"Here is it! Troll extraction," Jackson said. The three of them dove straight into the Trollipedia reading up on what exactly needed to be done.

A few minutes had passed, and the group felt confident in their plan. They made eye contact with each other as if they had finished their tests early and were waiting to be excused.

"Smashing," Pablo said to confirm the end of their research session. "We need him distracted. Wouldn't want anyone to get hurt."

"I can talk to anyone about almost anything," Jenelle said. "I also know him personally."

"Are you certain you want to be a part of this mission?" Jackson asked. "It's dangerous."

"Mr. Rosas is a good man," she began to explain. "If it helps him then it must be done. Plus, we can't leave him with a troll living inside of him."

"You could be in our Ghost Guard!" Jackson said with excitement.

"Woah, woah, Jackson, we don't just throw out offers to join our elite crew," Pablo interjected. "We do need some trusted allies though. Membership can be discussed later. How about that?"

"However, you all want to spin it," Jenelle responded so that Jackson wasn't put in an awkward position. "But you will come to like me soon enough Pablo. The rebels always do."

Jenelle walked slowly around the side of the gym so she could determine the best possible place to approach Officer Rosas. She felt that speaking to him from below the stage would be best as he wouldn't see what was taking place behind him. She cut through the middle of the crowd.

"Mr. Rosas, sir. Hello," Jenelle yelled, her voice echoing throughout the cafeteria. The kids closest to her got quiet and backed away, opening a direct path. Officer Rosas walked forward to the edge of the stage. Jackson and Pablo walked to the other side of the gym against the wall and made their way onto the stage just as Officer Rosas was turning away from them.

"Yes, Jenelle," he said, staring down at her. His voice was

heavier and raspier than she remembered. Jenelle was now directly beneath the stage in front of him. He motioned his head further downward.

"Well," she took a deep breath.

"I have some important information to share that my daddy told me to tell you if I happen to see you, and I didn't think you'd be in the school tonight, but it looks like you're here, which is perfect because he told me that you have been gaining a little weight," Jenelle continued trying to distract him. "Not in a bad way, you look um...hearty and he was wondering what it might be as he too wants to get stronger and more, ya know, thick," Jenelle continued rambling, which fully distracted Officer Rosas.

Pablo and Jackson made it to the back of the stage safely.

"You get on the mic, and I'll position myself behind the officer to pull the troll out of him," Pablo said.

Jenelle continued rambling on to keep Officer Rosas distracted. Jackson had the mic in hand and gave Pablo the hand sign to move forward. Pablo crept up quietly behind Officer Rosas like a video game character preparing for a stealth takedown. He held the mic stand firmly over his head.

Jenelle saw Pablo in position. She noticed Officer Rosas slightly turning around to check the perimeter, so she raised her voice a bit louder to reel him back in.

"So, what is it exactly?" Jenelle asked. "Like, a new workout routine? Did you get the BoFlex?"

CRACK!

The mic stand hit the back of Officer Rosas's head and he fell to the floor like a ton of bricks. The kids gasped loudly and approached the stage closer to see what might happen next.

"Listen up!" Jackson's voice crackled over the loudspeaker. He was standing on the right side of the stage with a microphone in hand.

"The town is in trouble," Jackson said. "This poor officer is being controlled by a troll! Well, the troll is inside with him. He's still this nice guy who barbecues for the neighbors but still isn't himself."

"What are you even saying?" said a kid in the audience as the others began chattering indistinctly.

"Show 'em, Pablo!" Jackson yelled into the mic, and the sound reverberated across the room. The crowd silenced.

Pablo stood directly over Officer Rosas and held the obsidian arrowhead necklace to his temple! The skin sizzled as it encountered the necklace. Pablo began to shake and was using all his strength at this point to keep the arrowhead in place. Officer Rosas began glowing purple from the temple as the color spread to every inch of his body. Pablo pressed harder and with his whole body. The ghost troll from inside began oozing out of Officer Rosas's temple! Pablo was lifted to a standing position as the ghost troll grew larger and larger out from the temple. The kids in the audience began to scream and yell.

"What the heck even is that?" someone yelled out.

"It's gonna eat us!" said another.

"Uh, guys? A little help here!" Pablo shouted. He struggled to contain the growing purple ghost troll which seemed to be just as knocked out as Officer Rosas. Jenelle jumped on stage and placed her hands on top of Pablo's to hold the necklace steady against the ghost troll. Her bangles and hoop earrings jiggled as if there were an earthquake.

"You see! These things are taking over our parents and want to eat us. They are hiding inside of the people we love. We must get out of here and stop them," Jackson yelled.

The kids cheered loudly.

"Let's do this!" a voice said.

"They aren't getting my momma. Let's mob out!" said another.

The ghost troll grew bigger and was now fully extracted from Officer Rosas's body. Jenelle and Pablo couldn't keep the ghost troll in place.

"They need your help!" Jackson yelled into the mic. "Climb on stage and help us vanquish the ghost troll." Jackson would have been right beside Pablo assisting him with the ghost troll extraction, but the plan was to have him be the voice of reason. The person to unite the crowd. They needed the facts.

A few of the kids close to the stage immediately climbed up to help. Suddenly more and more followed. Fifteen to twenty of Pablo's classmates were now surrounding him helping vanquish the ghost troll with only the small arrowhead necklace still sizzling the skin of the beast. The kids pushed, and the ghost troll fell off the stage, but no one stopped moving forward. Pablo, Jenelle, and ten other kids fell off the stage as well, their bodies smothering the ghost troll.

Pop!

The ghost troll combusted into a cloud of purple dust. The kids fell through the clouds directly onto the floor. Pablo and Jenelle lay at the bottom of the dog pile. Ten kinds fumbling to stand above them. The wind had been knocked out of Pablo and Jenelle, but no real damage occurred. The kids helped them up and brushed the purple dust off their backs.

Everyone cheered!

"Y'all did it!" shouted a girl standing nearby.

"Vaporized, fool!" said two boys watching from the side wall.

Officer Rosas began to awaken and touched the back of his head letting out a groan. He had a big gash, and blood was on his fingertips. Jenelle saw him from the corner of her eye and climbed onto the stage to check on him.

"What's going on? Where am I?" Officer Rosas said still disoriented from the blow to his head. He could not remember what had happened to him while the ghost troll inside of him controlled his body and mind.

"Rest here Mr. Rosas," Jenelle said. She grabbed some old costumes from the side stage and put them down so Officer Rosas could prop himself up a bit.

"You guys," Jenelle yelled to some of the kids conversing in the stage corner. "Get some stuff from the first aid box on the wall and help patch him up."

Pablo ran over to Jackson who was still standing on the side of the stage. Jackson thrust the microphone to Pablo's lips.

"You see!" Pablo yelled. "These things are trying to take over our town. Let's go out there and show them who lives here!! You may not understand this, but we need to march to the town square to shut down a portal that will end all of this! Are you with us?"

The kids cheered.

"He said... are you with us?" Jackson added to hype up the crowd even more.

The kids all cheered once again.

"Let's get the heck out of here!" someone yelled.

"Let's vaporize the purple people eaters!" another kid yelled.

"Save the town!" a girl said as she high fived her two friends on both sides of her.

"Then let's get out of here and march!! Grab whatever you can," Jackson yelled over the microphone.

The kids began to grab chairs and anything they could find in the gym. They sprung open the equipment closet and padded up with football and lacrosse gear.

"Let's battering ram the back door!" Pablo screamed.

The kids rammed the doors behind the stage and managed

to break the lock, but the doors still wouldn't fully open. They were being blocked by something. Pablo picked up the mic stand that he used to bash Officer Rosas with. He and Jackson then rushed to the door past all the other kids. Everyone used all their strength to push the doors open. They heard a big clunk, and the doors began to slowly open. A big dumpster had fallen on its side, trash spread out across the floor.

Pablo climbed to the top of the dumpster and looked back at the kids flowing through the doors.

"See!" Pablo yelled with the mic stand still in his right hand. The base rested flush with the floor. "They tried to trap us in here with this dumpster! But we broke free." He lifted his left hand high in the sky. The arrowhead necklace glimmered in the moonlight.

"This is our town, let's roll!" Pablo screamed.

Chapter 12: Reclaim the Town

The kids all marched the streets heading toward the town square. It was a dark cold night that seemed uninhabited since everyone was held indoors on lockdown. The air felt moist and the leaves on the street danced in the wind's breeze. They had about a mile to walk, and many started running. It may have been the excitement of it all or that some of the kids just needed to stay warm. Many of their costumes were not made to handle these frigid late-night conditions.

"It's freakin' freezing out here," an 11-year-old dressed in a ballerina costume said.

"You've got to be prepared for anything in this life, Breann," the girl beside her said. "That's why I'm dressed as a sandwich. It's warm and I'll never go hungry." The girl's mom made the costume from scratch. She has a cool DIY (do it yourself) costume every year.

Pablo, Jenelle, and Jackson were leading the crowd and still cheering from the exhilaration of the breakout. Everyone reached the middle of downtown and could see the center of the town square in the near distance.

Bright lights and sirens began to fill the night sky, but the kids marched forward unphased. Police cars, fire trucks, and ambulances pulled up swiftly in front of the statue, and police officers stood in front with their weapons drawn on the crowd of kids.

A voice came over the police car's loudspeaker, "You must stop now, or we will be forced to open fire. Please comply."

The army of kids stopped dead in their tracks looking at each other in fear.

"Would they really shoot us?" someone yelled in the crowd.

"I'm not trying to die tonight!" another girl in the crowd yelled hysterically as she grabbed her friend's hand pulling her toward the back of the crowd.

Pablo looked back and noticed the crowd's fear. He climbed on top of a parked car nearby and Jackson followed.

"Keep going, they won't hurt us!" Pablo yelled. "We are their food!"

A tall and stocky girl also in the 6th grade with long sandy blonde hair ran up to Jenelle who was standing beside the car.

"Hey, I found this in one of the cafeteria stage closets and figured it might be useful," the girl said, handing Jenelle a white and blue megaphone.

"Smart thinking," Jenelle said. "Cool costume too! What's

your name?"

"I'm Casey. Nice to meet you," she said.

Casey wore purple tights, bright clean white shoes, yellow leg warmers, turquoise gym shorts, and a vibrantly colored windbreaker. A pop of lime green from the wrist and headbands brought the 80s aerobics costume together.

Casey was feared by everyone in her grade due to her size. She never considered herself a mean person but hardened over time given all the bullying she had to put up with. People always called her a boy and treated her as such. She played recreational volleyball and was already on track to join the high school varsity team come freshman year. She was one of the most skilled middle-blockers in her age group. She lived with her aunt and uncle outside of town. They owned one of the most successful Christmas tree farms in the area. She spent most of her time training for volleyball or working for the family business. This left little time for growing lasting friendships. It seems she and Jenelle had similar experiences which is probably why they connected so seamlessly in that moment.

"Nice to meet you too," Jenelle said. "Hey, stay close by. This is about to get dangerous."

"Ok, sure! Sure, yeah you betcha," Casey responded as she backed away slowly. Her hand automatically gave Jenelle a thumbs up. "You betcha, Casey. Such a dork. Play it cool," she said to herself silently. Her nose and cheeks were bright red from the cold and half of her face was covered by her sweaty blonde hair that was no longer being kept up by the green headband. She adjusted the headband and wiped the sweat from her face. She was now prepared for anything.

Jenelle jumped on top of the car to join the others and switched on the megaphone.

"Listen up! Jackson has something to say," Jenelle yelled through the megaphone.

Jackson grabbed the megaphone firmly and nodded his head in gratitude. There was an obvious fondness for one another every time they spoke.

"You saw that ghost troll almost eat us!" Jackson yelled. "They are hungry, and we are their entrees! Those things are controlling the police. They won't shoot their food. Help us march forward and buy us a little time to save the town!"

Pablo put his arm around Jackson and pulled him close.

"For freedom!!" Pablo yelled through the megaphone.

Jenelle put her arm around both boys. "And justice!" she yelled.

The three looked at each other and at the same time belted

out, "For all!"

A few of the kids in the crowd caught on to the chant and shouted it out along with them.

Jackson and Pablo jumped down from the top of the car and stood in front of the other kids.

Jenelle saw Casey still standing beside the car and invited her up.

"Don't shoot, we're your food!" Jenelle yelled with Casey following along. "Don't shoot, we're your food!" Everyone was now chanting along. The girls jumped down from the car to join Jackson and Pablo.

"Very provocative! I like it," Jackson said.

"It needs work, but it gets the point across," Jenelle responded, bumping shoulders with him.

"Charge!" Jenelle yelled through the megaphone. The kids began to run forward, colliding directly with the officers and firefighters. A few school buses approached parking on the sides of the crowd. The officers began picking up kids and throwing them inside the buses.

"Aw!" Casey screamed. A firefighter grabbed her from behind and dragged her to one of the buses.

"We are experiencing a terrorist attack," the firefighter said. "You are not safe here."

Jenelle heard the commotion and ran to rescue Casey. She readied her stance and kicked him directly in the shins. Casey fell to the floor free of his grasp. Jenelle helped her up quickly and they ran to reconnect with Jackson and Pablo. They had finally arrived at the town square statue. It was a large fountain made from concrete, silver, and gold. A miner on a horse dressed in overalls and mining gear stood atop a platform surrounded by water. The left arm of the miner was outstretched high in the air. It looked to be holding some type of stone. The right hand was clenching a mining pick. The miner seemed to be in an attack position.

"This status is where the final portal lies," Jackson said.

"There must be some type of entrance somewhere," Pablo added. "Everyone, look around."

Casey searched around the outside of the statue, and the other three climbed over the ledge and into the water. They made their way to the center of the statue. Pablo and Jackson checked over the horse while Jenelle studied the base of the horse's stage for clues. Jackson was directly beneath the horse and knocked on its platform base. It made a hollow sound and appeared to have some type of door.

"Hey, I found the entrance," Jackson said. He was on his hands and knees inspecting its seams. "We just have to figure out how to open it."

Pablo climbed on top of the horse and sat right behind the miner figure. He noticed that the miner's hand had a crack around its wrist. He grabbed the rock in its hand and pulled it downward. The gears within the statue began to make a shifting sound.

"Aw!" Jackson screamed as he fell down the door he had been inspecting. His scream grew fainter as he slid further down into the darkness.

"Jackson!" Jenelle yelled now peering down the open trapdoor.

"Oh shoot, where did he go?" Pablo asked, still holding onto the miner's hand. He was frozen solid with fear of what might have happened to Jackson.

"He fell down there," Casey said. "Underneath the horse. He just dropped down. Disappeared."

Pablo climbed down from the horse like a chimpanzee. He peered down the hatch but couldn't see anything.

"Do you think he's going to be okay?" Jenelle said in a frantic voice. She had been so composed before but was obviously more worried now because it was Jackson.

"I'll go after him," Pablo said.

He grabbed Jenelle firmly and looked deep into her eyes. "You stay here and help everyone else. Be the leader you were meant to become." He had heard the line from an old adventure movie and knew it was the right moment to repeat it.

Jenelle shook her head and tried to compose herself. "Okay, I can do this. Make sure he's all right and be safe." She threw her wet arms over him. He hugged her back as if they had been friends for years.

"Find my sister, Carmen," Pablo said. "Tell her where to find us! She looks like me but prettier...and with long hair. You know, taller. In some uncomfortable cat costume. She is probably with a big football-looking guy named Dominik! He's alright I guess."

"Yes, yes go!" Jenelle said, rushing him off. "It's a small town. I know who Dominik the star football player is."

Pablo looked down into the trap door, "Look out adventure, the Pablo's coming for ya." He slid headfirst on his belly down some type of handmade tunnel slide. It felt rickety and dangerous like it came from an unknown small-town water park. He could see a reflection of light at the bottom but couldn't make out what it was. The slide had so many twists and turns. The light was actually a reflection from a small creek that lay beneath the slide's end. Pablo landed directly into it, SPLASH, went his body as he belly-flopped and sank close to the 10-foot bottom of the creek. He floundered a bit underwater and came to the surface for a big gasp of air. He climbed out of the creek and shook himself off. His mining helmet now rested at the bottom of the creek.

The area was dark and damp. Water continuously dripped from the fountain above. He figured only Frankie could have been behind creating such a cool slide entrance. It was probably a troll trap. Scary but thrilling, Pablo thought. He heard a screech and Jackson's voice followed.

"Pablo! Follow the li..." Jackson yelled but he could barely hear him.

"Jackson!" Pablo yelled.

He tried to refocus his eyes in the dark by closing them tightly and then reopening them. He desperately needed his eyes to adjust faster. He continued walking forward, trying to find the nearest wall, and bumped into what seemed to be a tool bench. He rustled around blindly grasping for anything he could find. His raincoat felt heavy and sticky from all the water. He took it off and flung it over the tool bench. He reached his hands out across the bench and came across a mining helmet. He fastened it tightly to his head, turning on the light. He scanned the room for any dangers and noticed the overall cleanliness.

The ground was dirt and rocks with no real plant life. It was a large, empty space with the creek in the center, surrounded by cave rocks. Frankie had definitely been down here handling the upkeep. A pickaxe lay on the bench, and he grasped it in his right hand ready for battle.

A large thud came from the distance, and Jackson's voice ricocheted through the rocks, "Pabl…"

"Have to hurry," Pablo said to himself rushing toward a narrow path where he could see purple light in the distance.

He climbed through the rocks as the light grew brighter. He checked his watch and had just fifteen minutes to close the portal. The path started to open, and he began to descend. He looked down the slope and could see the purple light glowing. He closed his eyes tightly to refocus. When he opened them there lay Jackson in the far-off distance face down in the dirt.

"Jackson!" Pablo yelled as he hurried down the slope trying not to trip on the loose rocks.

"Wake up! I'm coming! Hold on!" Pablo yelled.

Jackson lay silent in the dirt at the bottom of the slope. Pablo crouched down next to him, dropped the pickaxe, and turned him on his side to see if he was okay. Pablo held his cold wet hand in front of Jackson's mouth and could feel the warmth of his breath. Jackson was thankfully still alive.

Just then, Pablo felt a sharp kick to his abdomen which launched him into the air. He landed alongside the portal with his right foot smacking against it. His foot sunk into the portal like quicksand. He tried to pull his leg free, but it was being tugged on from the other side of the portal. It felt as if large hands were grasping at his calf. The pressure continued and he jolted his leg in pain as claws punctured his calf and shin at the same time. He grabbed his legs with both hands tugging to break free but could not break free from its clutches. At this moment, he suddenly remembered being flung across the room and wondered by what. He turned his head to the left and the ghost troll was lunging directly at him. It grabbed him by the chest and lifted him from the ground toward its mouth. Pablo was now being pulled between the unknown claws inside the portal and the ghost troll that lay in front of him. He squirmed but was unsure of which direction he'd rather succumb to. Unknown hands clawing at his pant legs, cutting into his skin, or the ghost troll in front of him preparing to swallow him headfirst. The ghost troll began to get angry and let out a roar.

Carmen found her way into the caverns, thanks to Jenelle's instructions, and heard the roar. She vaulted off the rocks and down the slope as fast as she could, her cat ears and tail dancing in the wind.

"Pablo!" she yelled, hoping for some type of answer.

"Yes, sis!" Pablo casually responded as if it were any other time that she called for him. His humorously calm expression was as if he weren't currently at odds with being ripped apart by two ferociously hungry ghost trolls.

She was now at the entrance to the area and saw Jackson lying motionless on the floor. She ran to him and saw her brother illuminated by the portal light being mangled by the ghost troll.

"Dominik, this way. I found them!" Carmen yelled as she raced toward Pablo.

The ghost troll tugged at Pablo trying to bring him to its mouth for consumption. Carmen saw the pickaxe beside Jackson and grabbed it with determination.

"No one better try to eat my brother without tasting what I have to offer first," Carmen said as she wound up the pickaxe and swung it directly into the temple of the ghost troll. His head popped like a dust-filled pimple and spread throughout his body, finally releasing Pablo from its grasp. Carmen dropped down to make sure he was all right.

"You saved me," Pablo said.

Carmen pulled him into her arms. They embraced each other caringly. Unfortunately, the unknown creature on the other end of the portal had never let go of Pablo's leg and pulled him swiftly closer to the portal. Carmen held on to him tightly using all her might to pull him back. The portal was not fully opened so pulling him through it was much harder for the unknown creature on the other side. Carmen lost her grip and the creature pulled Pablo completely through the portal. He shot his hand out and Carmen grasped it with both hands still pulling to bring him back.

"Carmen!" Dominik yelled. He made it down the slope and saw her crouched in front of the portal.

"Help me, Dominik," she said, still grasping Pablo's hand with all her strength. "Something is pulling him on the other side."

"I'm here," he said next to her grabbing Pablo's hand.

Pablo, now almost fully in the underworld portal, could see everything that lay ahead. A dark fiery world with lava streams and lost souls flying about. He looked to his feet and a troll was still pulling strong. It had two other trolls behind it pulling as well. This was one tug-of-war competition that these trolls did not want to lose. Pablo looked in the distance straight ahead and saw the army of Trolls, billions of them ready to enter but they weren't in ghost-like form. Pablo wondered how they might pass through the portal if they didn't have the ghost's ability. In the center tied to a wooden chair of some sort was Frankie, alive, but wounded. He was squirming to break free and one of the trolls smacked him in the back of the head to stop moving.

Pablo called out his name, "Frankie!" but he couldn't hear him. Pablo grew weak and felt defeated. His arm grew limp in Carmen and Dominik's hands. He was ready to accept his fate. These trolls were bound to rip him away from them like a brand-new doggy chew toy.

"He's not moving anymore," Carmen said, scared of what that might mean. "Dominik, his hand is limp. What does that mean?" She grew more frantic and shook Pablo's hand to see if he'd respond. Pablo did not move.

"I'm going in," Dominik said.

"No, no you can't," Carmen said. "We don't know what's in there. Let's just pull him harder. Maybe he passed out."

"Hold onto him tightly," Dominik told Carmen. "I'm going to let go and get him out of there."

"But wait," Carmen said. "Are you sure?"

"Yes," Dominik said. He took a few steps back to get a running start and ran swiftly leaping through the portal. He emerged on the other side above Pablo with his right fist in front of his body making direct contact with the face of the troll holding tight to Pablo's legs. All three trolls collapsed to the floor, releasing Pablo from their grasp. Dominik gained his balance after the hit and stood tall puffing his chest out. The troll army held its place about 20 yards away. It was as if they were waiting for some type of command. He locked eyes with the leader of the pack, and they began sprinting toward the portal. Dominik turned around quickly helping Pablo up and they jumped through the portal together.

"Pablo!" Carmen yelled. "You are safe. I can't believe you made it out of there. How's your leg?"

"I'm fine, sis. Really. We need to seal up the portal before they come through," Pablo said.

Carmen grabbed the light positioning it toward the portal and Pablo held up his necklace. The portal was now slowly hardening over. They could hear the yells and screams from inside the portal. The trolls from within banged at the door but could no longer break through.

Dominik looked confused. "Wait, why can't they all enter? That troll army was right behind us."

"They are dead," Pablo said, still holding the necklace in place. "They can't come to the land of the living unless it's through a ghost. Grab that pickaxe."

"Well, they seemed to be ready for something. As if they were about to go to war," Dominik said.

Dominik grabbed the pickaxe and put its tip next to the necklace. Pablo shined the mining helmet light at both items and a green beam of light shot out at the portal. It quickly hardened over fully. They had shut down the final portal and saved the town from a ghost troll infestation at last. They paused for a minute to breathe and began celebrating all together hugging and cheering until they remembered Jackson. They rushed over to him as he lay unconscious on the floor.

"Is he alive?" Carmen asked anxiously.

"Yes, he's still breathing," Pablo claimed as he once again checked for his warm breath against his fingertips.

Dominik lifted Jackson gently and placed him over his shoulder. They then made their way back up the slope. They were back at the creek and Pablo searched for another way up.

"Pablo, there's a ladder right over here…" Carmen said to him as if he had forgotten. "You actually thought I slid down that slide into that pool of water?"

"This is why you are my older sister. I was about to climb up the slide I came down," Pablo said.

They made their way up the ladder which was right next to the hatch slide. Dominik climbed slowly given he still had an unconscious Jackson nestled over his left shoulder.

"Well, ya know, I still would have chosen the slide even if I had known there was a ladder next to it," Pablo said as he climbed.

"And we would expect nothing less, great troll detective," Carmen said. She was almost at the top.

A battle was no longer raging above ground. All the parents had shown up and united with their kids. The police chief and mayor were waiting at the front of the statue. They saw Carmen emerge first and called the firefighters to help her out of the fountain water. Two firefighters climbed into the fountain walking toward Carmen.

"Do you need any assistance, Miss?" The towering brawny firefighter said to Carmen.

"Well, I was hoping to stay dry in all this so sure," Carmen responded. The firefighter lifted her up and carried her through the water to the edge of the fountain.

Pablo emerged next. "Carmen, they are the enemy. Don't let them help you."

"Relax, bro," Carmen said. "Things seem to be back in order now."

Pablo jumped into the fountain water and made his way toward the edge to join Carmen.

Dominik and an unconscious Jackson poked their heads out

and the firefighter assisted with carrying Jackson to the ambulance.

The chief of police met Pablo with open arms. He had Jenelle's megaphone in hand and addressed the crowd.

"Everyone, may I have your attention?" he said. "This little gentleman here, along with his friends, saved our town from the paranormal terrorist attack that overtook many of our officers and students."

Pablo looked confused and shook his head in disbelief. Dominik put his arm over Carmen and they both smiled. Pablo's eyes looked toward the ambulance as he saw Jackson being loaded up. Jackson's grandfather climbed in after him. Pablo looked around for Jenelle and Casey but couldn't find them.

Everything seemed to be okay, but he had this feeling in the pit of his stomach that no one could be trusted. Did shutting down the last portal kill off all the remaining ghost trolls? Or were they now just in hiding? He needed Jackson. He was the yin to his yang.

"How does it feel to be a hero, young man?" the mayor asked Pablo.

"The hero-ing isn't done yet, I can tell you that much," said a skeptical Pablo.

The mayor yanked Pablo closer, shaking him in congratulations.

"The paranormal threat has been contained, everyone," said the mayor over the megaphone. "We can all return to our homes and sleep soundly. We will release more information in the morning."

"Pablo, we did it," Carmen said to him.

"Then why are all my friends missing?" Pablo asked.

"Little bro, you only have one friend, not including me," Carmen said.

"There were two girls. They helped us," Pablo responded.

"Oh, ladies' man," Dominik said. "We will help you find them later buddy. Let's get you home before you get sick from those wet clothes."

Carmen put her arms out wide waiting for a hug from Pablo. He looked at her with a smirk and nestled himself into her arms. Dominik put his arm around her and embraced them both in happiness.

Chapter 13: That's my Best Friend

The next morning, Pablo awoke to the aroma of bacon and nearly burnt hash browns. He rushed downstairs to find Carmen and his *papá*, Martin cooking.

"Good morning there, hero! Sit down and eat with us," Martin said enthusiastically. He knew his kids would get into some type of trouble without him being home, but he had never imagined this.

Pablo sat down next to Carmen at the kitchen table, and she elbowed him playfully, smirking with amusement. He acted as if she hurt him and let out a sound signifying intense pain.

"Owww..." he groaned, smirking back at her.

The news came on over the living room TV that could be slightly seen from the kitchen table. The newscaster began to share the details of last night informing viewers that a supernatural terrorist attack was ultimately destroyed by Pablo and his friends. They didn't mention any other names, just his.

"Can we turn that off? They are misrepresenting the facts," Pablo said, focusing his attention on the glass of orange juice in front of him. He took a big swig while holding the glass with two hands.

Carmen turned off the TV and grabbed her iPod from the counter. "I know you prefer music over listening to random people talk," Carmen said. "As do I," she continued, handing him one of her headphones.

"What is this?" Pablo asked, surprised. "Has a ghost troll taken over your body? This is not your usual sound trend."

"Stop," she said, nudging him as her cheeks grew pink. "It's 'Everywhere,' by Fleetwood Mac. It's easy listening after a wild night."

"Oh my gosh, you freakin' like him?" Pablo joked.

"Carmen likes who?" Martin asked as he held a hot skillet in his right hand with an oven mitt on the other.

"So, you want to go see Jackson after this?" Carmen asked Pablo, avoiding her father's question. "You'll probably feel much better about everything if you are by his side."

"You really get me," Pablo said.

"I get that you need to eat to figure out whatever it is that is troubling you," Martin said as he put the finishing touches on their breakfast plates.

"Affirmative," Pablo said in a robotic voice.

"A feast for my two great heroes," Martin said proudly as he set down their plates filled with eggs, bacon, hashbrowns, guacamole, and tortillas.

"*Gracias, Papá! Mi favorito,*" Pablo said.

"*Gracias, Papá,*" Carmen added.

"We will all go check in on Jackson this evening," Martin said.

Jackson lay unconscious on the hospital bed. His room was plain white with a large window. The day was gloomy and dark gray clouds filled the sky. Some light managed to peek through the blinds.

Pablo and Carmen arrived at the open door. Martin met with Jackson's grandfather in the lobby.

"Hi, best buddy," Pablo said sadly to a motionless Jackson hooked up to hospital devices. Pablo held a large duffle bag on his shoulder.

Carmen put her hand on his back and pushed him a bit to enter the room. Pablo walked slowly to Jackson's bed staring down at his shoes. He dropped the duffle bag at the foot of the bed and stopped for a moment. He didn't want to cry in front of Jackson, so he tried not to look at him. He sat in the chair next to Jackson's bed staring deeply into the crisp white sheets that kept Jackson warm. He grabbed the sheet with both hands feeling the fabric to distract himself, but it didn't help. His eyes filled with tears, but he tried to hold them back. His nose filled with mucus, and he sniffled as a teardrop fell from his right eye down to his hand. His face grew heavy, and his bottom lip began to puff out as he sobbed quietly.

Carmen stood at the door debating on whether to enter and console him or give him his space.

"Monkey, I have to help *Papá* with something," Carmen said. It was a lie, but she knew Pablo needed this moment alone with Jackson. "You okay here?" She was also on the verge of bawling her eyes out. Her emotions would take over if she stayed any longer.

Pablo looked up from the sheets and turned his head to the left barely past his shoulder. He did not want to make direct eye contact with her so stared off into the distance nodding his head yes.

"I'll be back for you soon," Carmen said as she left the open doorway, her eyes now heavy with tears.

Pablo's head stayed in the same position for a moment. He tried to collect himself before looking back at Jackson. He grabbed the hood of his sweatshirt with his left hand to dry off his tears and clear the mucus from his nose. He moved his attention toward Jackson and sighed deeply.

"I'm sorry for opening the trap door," he whispered, still trying to stop himself from bawling uncontrollably.

"We were supposed to stick together. If you don't make it then I don't know how I am going to live with myself," Pablo said.

He stayed quiet for a few seconds thinking about how hard everything would be without Jackson. How lucky he was to have made such a great friend. Their adventures had just begun and were already so epic.

"I'm going to be here with you until you wake up. And I'm definitely going to fix this ugly boring room because you just don't deserve mediocrity, as you would say about me," Pablo explained, chuckling a bit.

"Amigos for life," Pablo said as he put out his right fist with his thumb extended to meet Jackson's motionless fist.

"Pew," Pablo whispered as he launched his thumb outward like a rocket.

Jackson extended his left fist with his thumb extended to meet Pablo's and upon connection, they launched it outwards like a rocket.

Pablo got up from the chair and unpacked the duffle bag. He

had a few of Jackson's favorite things and wanted to make him seem more at home. The first thing he added was a twin-sized Teenage Mutant Ninja Turtles comforter to the bed. He placed it over Jackson and began fixing the sides to tuck him in. He then pulled out the mining helmet that he had worn the previous night as well as a mattock.

"We have to keep you safe, buddy. So, I'm going to put the helmet on the bedside table. That way you can turn it on to see at night if you hear anything creepy. The mattock probably isn't allowed in here, but these are desperate times. I'm going to hide it under your mattress for emergencies," Pablo said as he showed the items to an unconscious Jackson before placing them in each location.

"I know you'd ask me how I got the mattock past security if you were here. And the answer is...I told them I crapped my pants upon arrival, so they let me run to the bathroom! I handed the bag off to Carmen and they forgot all about it," Pablo said, now laughing to himself.

"Works every time," Pablo said.

He continued placing other fun items around the room and began writing notes in his composition book. He wanted to have a plan down by the time Jackson awoke. Carmen entered the room and put her hand on Pablo's shoulder.

"Pablo," Carmen said to him in a calming whisper. "Let's get you home."

"Can I please stay here? He is probably going to wake up in the middle of the night scared wondering what happened," Pablo explained.

"You know *Papá* is not going to like you staying here overnight. I gotta get you home," she said, embracing him in a soft hug.

"I just escaped death multiple times, what's the worst that could happen to me staying here?" Pablo pleaded.

"Fine, but please do actually sleep. I'll make you a comfy chair bed," Carmen said.

She grabbed some sheets and pillows from the closet and put the two chairs together to form a bed. Pablo made his way to the bed and got comfortable.

"Music will keep you safe," she said, putting her iPod on his chest and an ear pod into his right ear. She has already queued up a song for him. Pablo immediately recognized the song and images of his mother singing it in the kitchen popped into his mind.

"Cuz I'm dreaming of you tonight, 'til tomorrow, I'll be holding you tight," Pablo sang along quietly to himself.

"Mom's favorite song," Carmen whispered.

"'Dreaming of You,' by Selena," they said together at the same time. She kissed him on the forehead.

"Love you, Monkey. I'll be here at 8 am sharp."

"Love you too. I'll be fine. Jackson is with me."

She left the room and he fell asleep dreaming of his mother.